Haven *of* Obedience

Also by Marina Anderson

Dark Secret
Forbidden Desires
The Discipline

Haven *of* Obedience

MARINA ANDERSON

sphere

SPHERE

First published in Great Britain in 2000 by X Libris
Reprinted 2002, 2003, 2005, 2007, 2009 (twice)
This paperback edition published in 2012 by Sphere
Reprinted 2012 (five times)

A CIP catalogue record for this book
is available from the British Library.

ISBN 978-0-7515-5051-1

Typeset in Sabon by M Rules
Printed and bound in Great Britain by
Clays Ltd, St Ives plc

Papers used by Sphere are from well-managed forests
and other responsible sources.

MIX
Paper from
responsible sources
FSC
www.fsc.org FSC® C104740

Sphere
An imprint of
Little, Brown Book Group
100 Victoria Embankment
London EC4Y 0DY

An Hachette UK Company
www.hachette.co.uk

www.littlebrown.co.uk

Haven *of* Obedience

Chapter One

On a Sunday night in April, twenty people were assembled in the reception area of The Haven. Rob Gill, the owner, was addressing them as they listened attentively. 'I trust you've enjoyed your stay over the past three days,' he said, a half-smile playing around his lips. 'At the very least I'm sure that you've all learned something new about yourselves.'

Jan Pearson, a twenty-eight-year-old freelance casting director, felt herself start to blush. She glanced at the rest of the group, all of whom were watching Rob. They looked so conventional now: the women in their trouser suits or designer leisure clothes, most of the men smartly suited. This was in sharp contrast to the way they'd looked over the past weekend. For example, she'd last seen the man standing next to her – now safely encased in his three-piece suit, white shirt and dark blue tie – kneeling submissively at the feet of a voluptuous blonde, his hands tied behind his back as he waited, trembling with excitement and need, for her finally to allow him a cruelly delayed climax.

'What it's important for you to understand,' continued Rob, 'is that you are now part of a very select and secret society. When you arrived here you signed a form, swearing to keep our code of silence. You may find this difficult once you start mixing with friends from your everyday life again. But if any of you should break your vow, then you will be ostracised. In other words, you won't be allowed to visit us again.'

Jan's mouth went dry. Even after just one weekend she was addicted to the pleasures that she'd learned to enjoy here, at this very special retreat. If anyone had told her how erotic she'd find it to be forced into obedience and submission she would have laughed at them. In all her relationships she'd been in control, and that was the way she'd liked it. However, her stay at The Haven had changed her completely.

Rob was still speaking. 'I'm sure that many of you

here today will want to stay in touch with each other, and that's how we like it. You're all like-minded people now. The only people here that you're not free to continue seeing are any of your tutors. You have to remember that for us this is a job of work. It isn't personal.'

The nipples beneath Jan's V-necked, semi-fitted ribbed cardigan suddenly stiffened and she felt the caress of the material against the rigid tips. It was Rob's fault – his words had reminded her of the previous evening.

She'd been lying on her bed in an exhausted, sated heap after a long session with one of the other tutors and two of the guests when Rob had entered the room. He'd been accompanied by a trainee tutor, a young lad who hadn't had anything to do with Jan before her visit. Rob had told her that they were there to pleasure her for an hour. At first she thought there'd been a mistake, and she'd explained that she'd already been very well pleasured. It was then that his expression had changed, changed to one that she'd become used to over the weekend. His piercing blue eyes had narrowed.

'I hope you're not still trying to tell me what to do,

Jan?' Rob had asked. Remembering the punishments she'd endured before she'd come to understand the rules of The Haven, Jan had hastily shaken her head. 'That's good,' he'd continued. 'Because as you know, here you're expected to be obedient to our wishes. It's Marc and I who wish to pleasure you: *your* wishes are of no importance.'

To Jan's surprise, Rob's words had excited her. All the same, she had felt certain that her tired body would be unable to respond no matter what the two men did. How wrong she'd been, she thought now as memories of the intense orgasms that they'd wrenched from her rushed through her mind.

Jan recalled the way Rob had sat astride her, his hands kneading her breasts with sweet-scented oil, while Marc had kneeled at the foot of the bed, parting her legs and using his tongue with incredible skill on the soft centre of her. She'd lost count of the number of times her body had contorted, arching upwards in spasm after spasm of helpless pleasure. It had been an incredible experience, and when Rob had finally climbed off her and run a hand over her sweat-streaked flesh she'd thought that for a brief moment there had been something personal in his gaze. Now it seemed that she'd been wrong. Or, even if she was right, she would never be able to find out.

'I hope that we'll see you here again some time,' said Rob as his speech drew to a close. 'I suggest that those of you who've learned that there can be pleasure through pain should exchange phone numbers. For most of you, your new sexual preferences might come as something of a shock to the people you've previously been intimate with.' A ripple of uneasy laughter spread through the room.

Jan's buttocks clenched beneath her ankle-length pencil skirt as she recalled the hot, stinging sensation caused by the latex whip, wielded so expertly by Simon, Rob's second-in-command. She'd cried out with shock and anger the first time it had happened to her. But as she'd been spreadeagled on a large wooden table, her wrists and ankles held firmly by other guests, she'd been unable to do anything about it.

Slowly, as her 'punishment' had continued, she'd been surprised to realise that the discomfort quickly passed whilst the heat from the lashes seemed to race through her flesh, causing her breasts to burgeon and her belly to swell. Yes, she must certainly exchange some telephone numbers before she got into her car and set off again for London, and her busy work schedule.

'And now it's time for you all to go,' said Rob, with a smile. 'Remember everything you've learned here. You don't want to waste your money, do you?' Again there was laughter, but this time it wasn't embarrassed laughter. Jan tried to catch Rob's eye for a moment, wanting to prove to herself that she'd been right and that she was special to him. But without another word he turned and left the room. With a start she realised that the crotch of her panties was damp. Just thinking about the things that had happened to her had excited her again.

A man of about Jan's own age approached her. She remembered him from the Saturday. He'd been an amazingly adept lover, although at that stage she still hadn't mastered how to hand over control completely. Now that she had, sex with him would probably be even better so when he asked if she'd like to give him her phone number she accepted eagerly.

'I was thinking of having a party some time soon,' she told him.

'That's a good idea. I hope I'll be on the guest list.'

Jan smiled, tucking her short, sleek brown hair

behind her ears. 'I thought eight would be an ideal number. What do you think?'

He nodded. 'Yes, eight sounds about right. It's been an interesting weekend, hasn't it?' He stared intently at her.

A shiver ran through her. 'Very interesting,' she said softly. As he touched the side of her face lightly with his fingers Jan remembered the way the same fingers had forced her hands above her head, and how his mouth had fastened around her left nipple, sucking cruelly at the delicate skin as he ignored her protests – because that was what the weekend was all about. Suddenly she wanted him again, there and then, and she could see from the look in his eyes that he knew it.

'Don't wait too long before you ring,' he commanded her. Whereas before her stay at The Haven she would have resented his tone, now it excited her.

'I won't,' she assured him. Then, reluctantly, Jan picked up her cases and began the journey back to London.

Chapter Two

By the time Natalie Bowen arrived home at her small but expensive flat on the outskirts of London it was nearly nine o'clock. A tall, slim and typically cool English blonde, she realised that she was in danger of having nothing in her life apart from her magazine. Admittedly the magazine was a great achievement. She'd started it eighteen months earlier, deliberately targeting women in the twenty-five-to-thirty-five age group, single and working in high-powered jobs. She felt that most magazines were trying to teach women how they could juggle home, children and work, but she wasn't interested in the home-and-children side. She dealt with fashion, health and relationships, both in and out of the workplace, and the magazine's success had exceeded even her expectations.

All of which was very pleasing. But somehow, despite all the articles in her magazine aimed at helping women like her, Natalie had got lost. Her tendency to be impatient, and her ability to cut straight to the heart of the matter, were assets at work – but not when it came to staying in a relationship. She had no trouble in attracting men, but was beginning to find little satisfaction in short-term affairs, which were pleasurable enough sexually but left her feeling empty.

'Do as the editor says, not as the editor does,' Natalie muttered to herself as she opened her front door. Glancing at the answerphone she was disappointed to see that no one had called while she was out. There were several people she half expected to hear from, including Philip, although she was beginning to suspect that she'd been politely ditched by him. But it was Jan she really wanted to ring her: Jan was her best friend and until a month ago they'd met up at least three times a week.

Because Jan too had a busy professional life and struggled to find a man that she considered good enough for herself, the two of them always had plenty to gossip about. Also, they shared the same sense of humour and the same love of Italian food and good wine. Natalie couldn't understand why Jan had stopped phoning her. It wasn't as though there'd been an argument, or even a disagreement. At their last meeting Jan had mentioned that she was going away the following weekend but had promised to call Natalie as soon as she'd got back. The call had never come.

Too tired to cook herself anything, Natalie took a bottle of wine from the fridge and poured herself a large glass. Then she chopped up some feta cheese in a bowl, threw in some black olives and some tomatoes and sat down in front of the television. After the meal her hand started to move towards the phone. Then she drew it back again. She didn't know why, but she was reluctant to call Jan herself. There had to be a reason for her friend's silence and she wasn't sure that she wanted to know it, not if Jan was going to end their friendship.

It was only after two more glasses of wine that she finally found the courage to dial the number. The phone rang for a long time. She was about to hang up when Jan answered.

'Hi!' Her familiar voice was slightly breathless, as though she'd had to hurry to get to the phone.

'Jan? It's me, Nat.'

'Nat.'

There was an awkward pause, a pause that Natalie rushed to fill. 'Yes, you remember me, I'm the one whose shoulder you cry on when men disappoint you.'

'God, look, I'm really sorry I haven't rung you,' babbled Jan. 'The truth is I've been incredibly busy casting for a new historical drama. I haven't had a moment to myself for the past few weeks. I was going to ring you tonight, but I seem to have gone down with some kind of virus.'

Natalie frowned to herself. She thought that she could hear people in the background, people laughing and chattering. But it was always possible it was the television that Jan had put on to cheer herself up. 'How was your weekend away?' she asked brightly.

'What weekend away?'

'You know, the one you took just after we last met. You told me you were going to a retreat or something like that. What was it like? Did it do you any good?'

'It was all right,' said Jan hesitantly.

12

'What do you mean, "all right"? I got the impression it was going to be something special.'

'Did you? I don't know why. It was just a weekend in the country.'

Natalie knew that Jan wasn't telling her the truth. 'If you say so,' she said stiffly, annoyed at being lied to. 'Well, shall I come round and see you tomorrow? I'll bring some chicken soup and grapes.'

'No, you can't come tomorrow,' said Jan. Now she sounded panic-stricken.

'Why not? You're not infectious, are you?'

'My mother's coming over.'

'From Paris? You really must be ill.' Natalie could hear that she was getting an edge to her voice and she knew that Jan must be able to hear it too.

'Look, I can't talk now,' said Jan, suddenly lowering her voice. 'We'd better meet after work one night next week.'

'How about Tuesday?' suggested Natalie.

'No, sorry I can't do Tuesday, I've got some friends coming round.' 'Anyone I know?'

'No, people in the same line of business as me. I tell you what, Thursday's clear. I'll see you at our usual Italian place at seven o'clock, okay?'

'You're sure you can spare the time?' asked Natalie coolly. At that moment she heard a man's voice calling Jan. It was clear that he was impatient. 'It sounds as though the doctor's arrived,' Natalie said sharply. 'I'll see you on Thursday' With that she slammed down the phone. At least she'd made contact with Jan again, and it didn't sound as though she'd done anything to offend her. What hurt was the realisation that Jan suddenly appeared to be having a far busier social life than Natalie was. She'd have to ask Jan about that when they met.

Jan put her cordless phone down on the kitchen worktop. Natalie couldn't have rung at a worse time. She felt terrible about the way the conversation had gone, but she hadn't been able to say any more because Richard had been standing right behind her, listening to every word.

'Who was that?' he asked, running a finger down her spine.

Wearing only a black leather thong and high-heeled shoes, Jan felt incredibly vulnerable – which was how she was supposed to feel. It was also how she liked feeling, when she wasn't at work. That was what they'd taught her at The Haven, and they'd taught her well. 'No one you know,' she said lightly. 'Only a friend.'

'And is your friend pretty?' asked Richard, placing his hands on each side of her waist with his fingers splayed out over her belly.

'Yes, but she wouldn't interest you. She's a high-powered businesswoman who likes to be in control of her men.'

'Perhaps she should go to The Haven for a weekend,' murmured Richard, his voice growing husky with desire. 'We're going upstairs now and while I'm making love to you, you're going to describe her to me.'

'I am not!' retorted Jan.

She felt Richard's left hand move to the nape of her neck and he gripped her tightly. 'I hope you're not going to slip back into your old ways, Jan,' he whispered. 'Don't forget that the men are in charge here this weekend. As long as you do as we say, you receive as much pleasure as you can bear, remember?'

Her whole body tightened with desire. 'Of course I remember,' she whispered. Then she walked up the stairs in front of him, past other guests – some of whom reached out to caress her as she and Richard made their way to her bedroom. Once there she knew that soon,

MARINA ANDERSON

desperate to feel the delicious hot liquid pleasure rush through her, she would be doing as he'd said. She knew it was a betrayal of Natalie but, shamingly, the dark perversity of what she was about to do only increased her excitement.

Natalie arrived at Mario's before Jan. Watching her friend arrive she noticed that Jan was looking tense. When Natalie waved to her, Jan's answering smile seemed strained. 'Sorry I'm late,' she said breathlessly, sliding into the seat opposite Natalie. 'The damned casting session ran overtime, as usual.'

'I've only been here five minutes,' said Natalie. 'I've ordered a bottle of the house red for us but thought I'd wait for you before I ordered any food.'

'Fine,' said Jan vaguely. 'I'll have the spaghetti al pomodoro.' She then began to flick through her pocket diary.

Natalie decided to have the fresh pasta filled with spinach and ricotta in a tomato and basil sauce, her favourite meal at Mario's. Since Jan showed no inclination to eat she had to catch the waiter's eye and order for them both.

'Don't you ever get tired of having the same food?' asked Jan, putting her diary away.

16

Natalie shook her head. 'No, I know what I like.'

'I thought I did.' Jan's tone was strange.

'What do you mean?'

'Nothing. How's the magazine, then?'

'Taking up far too much of my life, as usual. Philip's dumped me, in case you wanted to know but didn't dare ask.'

Jan looked sympathetically at her. 'Bad luck. Did he say why?'

'Oh, the usual stuff about not wanting to get involved, feeling that I deserved someone better. It's not what he meant, of course. It went wrong the last time we had sex. I said that I wanted to be on top because my orgasms are always better that way and ...' She stopped as the waiter arrived and they both had to stifle their giggles. 'He must have missed us,' laughed Natalie as they began to eat. 'I'm sure no one else has such interesting conversations.'

'Go on with what you were saying,' commanded Jan.

'Oh, that. Yes, well, he didn't like me saying that I knew best. He pretended that it was all right, that he liked a woman who knew her own mind and understood her own body. But it put him right off.'

'You mean although you had a better time, he didn't?'

Natalie nodded. 'Exactly. God, the times that's happened to me. Still, it's happened to you too, hasn't it? That's some comfort to me. I'm not alone in this.'

'No,' murmured Jan.

'Is that all you've got to say? Haven't you got any interesting gossip for me? How's *your* sex life at the moment?'

'It's okay,' said Jan, with a shrug.

'What do you mean, "okay"? Are you seeing someone special?'

'No.'

'Are you seeing anyone at all?'

'Yes, now and again.'

'Is there some reason why you can't tell me about him?' asked Natalie. 'Is he married or something?'

'No, it's just that it isn't very interesting.'

Natalie couldn't believe her ears. 'Your sex life's *always* interesting. What's the matter? You're keeping something back from me, I know you are. Is this why you haven't rung me since your weekend away? Did you meet someone dishy there, someone you want to keep secret?'

'Oh Nat,' said Jan sadly. 'I wish I could tell you about it, but I can't.' She lowered her voice. 'You see, it isn't allowed.'

'Isn't *allowed?*' shouted Natalie.

'Ssh!'

'Why do you keep whispering and why have I got to keep my voice down? I don't understand what's happened to you,' said Natalie. 'You've changed completely since we last met. Have I offended you or something?'

'No, you haven't done anything,' said Jan firmly. 'Please, can we just change the subject?'

Natalie sighed. 'If that's what you want. But the evening won't be as much fun as usual. You'd better tell me about this place where you went for your weekend. You're looking really well, so it must have done you good. Perhaps I should go there. Where is it?'

'It's, uhm ... sort of in the country.'

'That's a *great* help. I should be able to find it easily from *that.*'

'I can't tell you where it is,' said Jan, the exasperation clear in her voice.

Never before had Natalie felt uncomfortable when

she was with Jan. They'd always been like sisters, able to talk about anything and everything. Obviously, for reasons known only to Jan, that was no longer the case. Suddenly Natalie just wanted the meal to be over and to escape back to her flat. She felt incredibly hurt. 'I think you'd better choose what we're going to talk about,' she snapped. 'Nothing that I pick seems to be right.'

'Nat, I *am* sorry,' responded Jan, leaning over the table towards her friend. 'I'd like to tell you, truly I would, but I'm not supposed to.'

'Then don't. Idon't think I want a pudding. Let's just have coffee and then split, shall we?'

'Oh, blow them,' said Jan. 'Listen, Nat.' She dropped her voice. 'I *will* tell you about my weekend away but you must never talk about it to anyone else. If you do, you're going to ruin everything for me. So will you promise me that before I start?'

Now Natalie was intrigued. 'Of course. You know me, I'm good at keeping secrets.'

'Yes, well you'd better be because I'm risking everything in telling you this. The place I went to was called The Haven. It's in Sussex. A girl at work told me about it. You see, they don't advertise. People have to hear of the place by word of mouth, and their names must be put forward by someone who's already been before they can actually go there to stay.'

'But why?' asked Natalie in astonishment. 'Do you have to be incredibly fit or something?'

'Hardly, or I wouldn't have got in. No, it's really a weekend seminar.'

'A business seminar? I don't want a weekend away working. I want a break.'

'It's a seminar in sex.'

Natalie couldn't believe her ears. 'What on earth do you mean?'

'Exactly what I say. People go there to learn how to fulfil their sexual potential, but it's a very special kind of potential. You see, it's for women like you and me, or for men who spend all their time controlling people at work. They teach you how to hand control over to your partner in order to gain your pleasure. I heard one of the tutors refer to it as "the haven of obedience", which sums it up.'

'I can't believe I'm hearing this right,' said an astonished Natalie. 'You're not telling me—'

'For heaven's sake keep your voice down.' Jan looked nervously around her.

'Sorry. You're not telling me that you became a submissive, are you?'

'Yes,' confessed Jan. 'It was incredibly difficult at first. To be honest, I didn't think that I was going to make it through the first day and night but I was determined to try. Let's face it, my sex life's hardly been that wonderful, running it the way I wanted to, so what did I have to lose? Anyway, once I started to give in and do what they wanted me to, it was so fantastic that I just wanted to learn more and more.'

'What do they make you do?'

Jan shook her head. 'Now that's something I *really* can't tell you.'

'I can understand that they might want to keep the place a secret,' said Natalie. 'What I don't understand is why I haven't heard from you since you got back.'

'Because I'm still seeing loads of the people who were at The Haven when I was. We have parties at each other's houses, and meet up for dinners that always turn into something rather more exciting. The trouble is, we're not allowed to invite people who've never been to The Haven, which is why I haven't been able to include you. The awful thing is, Nat, I've got so caught up in it that I can hardly bear to take an evening off even to see you, my best friend.'

Natalie could see that simply thinking about it was exciting Jan. Her cheeks were flushed, her eyes bright and her hand, gripping the stem of her wine glass, wasn't quite steady. Suddenly Natalie wanted to feel like that, to have something to be excited about – and, more to the point, to have truly satisfying sex. 'Do you think I could go there?' she asked.

Jan frowned. 'I honestly don't think you'd like it. I've rather simplified what goes on there. The place is very strictly run and if you don't do as you're told, well . . . ' Her voice trailed off.

'Well, what?' demanded Natalie.

'You get punished,' whispered Jan.

'Punished?'

'Yes. But even the punishments are designed to turn you on, only in a completely different way from anything you've ever experienced before. I really don't think it's for you, Nat.'

'I wouldn't have thought that it was for *you*. But you seem to have enjoyed it. Surely they'd take me if you put my name forward?'

'I suppose so, but I don't want to.'

Natalie felt as though her friend had slapped her. 'I think you're being incredibly selfish,' she said finally. 'You've been there and come back a totally different person. You admit that your sex life's now fantastic and that you're seeing people nearly every night of the week. Do you know what *I* do when I stop work each day? I go home, drink too much wine and go to bed with only the cat for company.'

'But if I did put you forward and then you didn't like it once you got there, it would reflect badly on me,' explained Jan. 'I don't want that to happen. I don't want to spoil what I've got, and they'll start questioning my judgement if I send the wrong person along.'

'I honestly can't see what can be so bad about the place,' said Natalie. 'I'm not some naïve eighteen-year-old. I'm twenty-seven, and I've had a fair bit of experience. I doubt if anything they suggest is going to shock me.'

'Oh Natalie, you have absolutely no idea of what I'm talking about, do you?' said Jan. 'You're the same as I was. You've always liked being in control, both at work and in bed. The older the pair of us got, the more dominating we became. That's why we frightened all

24

the men off, only neither of us realised it. At least, I know I didn't – not until I went to The Haven.'

'I accept all that,' replied Natalie. 'If you're truly my friend then prove it to me by putting my name forward. I promise I won't let you down, no matter how much of a shock I get.' She laughed.

Jan hesitated for a few more seconds and then shrugged. 'On your own head be it, then. The only thing is, knowing you, and knowing what it's like there, I want you to take the two-weekend option. I don't think you'd be able to put up with the intensive course.'

'Whatever you say,' agreed Natalie hastily. Privately she thought Jan had gone mad. She couldn't imagine any sexual situation where she wouldn't be able to cope. 'You'll do it, then? You'll put my name forward?'

'I've said I will, haven't I?'

For the first time in months Natalie felt excited about something other than her work. 'How long will it take before I hear from them?'

'I had to wait several weeks.'

Natalie groaned. 'Oh, no. I was looking forward to going next weekend.'

'They're booked up a long way ahead. Now I have to go. I've got someone coming round for the night.'

Natalie didn't mind any more, not now that she understood why Jan was so busy. Soon she would be as well. 'That's all right,' she said with a smile. 'Don't forget to ring them up about me tomorrow, will you?'

'No, I won't,' Jan assured her. As the pair of them stepped outside into the fresh air she glanced at Natalie. 'I really hope I'm doing the right thing for you,' she said slowly. 'If you don't like it, you won't hold it against me, will you?'

'I'm going to love it,' said Natalie confidently. 'I wanted my life to change, but I didn't know how to do it. Now you've solved the problem for me.'

'Give me a ring when you've finished the course,' said Jan, hailing a taxi.

'Aren't we going to meet again before then?' asked Natalie.

'No,' shouted Jan, climbing into the cab. 'I haven't got an evening free for the next two months.'

As the taxi sped away, Natalie shivered with a mixture of nerves and anticipation. She realised that Jan was right. She was more private than her friend, and the two-weekend option was probably the right one for her. She also realised that she'd now taken the first step on a journey that would lead her to discover new things about herself sexually. Unexpectedly, she was already aroused by the thought of learning to relinquish control and be dominated in bed. It was something that she would never have considered for a moment before hearing about The Haven from Jan and seeing what a difference it had made to her friend.

Chapter Three

Six weeks later Natalie was driving down a small country lane in Sussex, rapidly approaching The Haven. Now that she was nearly there she felt quite nervous. If it hadn't been for the fact that Jan had risked everything by putting her forward, she might have lost her nerve, turned round and returned to London. However, that wasn't an option. She had to go through with this. She only hoped that once her two weekends were over she'd be as happy and fulfilled as Jan was.

The Haven was a big old country house set in six acres of grounds. As Natalie parked her car in the courtyard round the back of the ivy-covered building, she saw a few people strolling in the summer sunshine.

Interestingly, they were all strolling alone: none of them seemed inclined to talk or mix. Pulling her suitcase and overnight bag out of the boot, she walked into the thickly carpeted reception area. Behind the desk a young auburn-haired girl was standing. She smiled at Natalie. 'Your name?' she asked.

'Natalie Bowen.'

The girl's eyes flicked down a printed list in front of her. 'Ah, yes.' Again the practised smile. 'You're in room sixteen. I'll show you the way.'

Natalie was surprised. She'd expected to be ushered into a large room and made to mix with a crowd of strangers immediately. Clearly she was quite wrong. At the moment this was no different from booking into an ordinary country hotel. 'Did you find us all right?' asked the girl, who was wearing a label that said her name was Sue.

'Yes, thank you. The directions I was sent were very good.'

'That's all right then. Here, I expect you'd like to freshen up before the evening meal.'

Now Natalie was even more surprised. 'Don't I get to meet any of the other guests first?' she asked.

'You can always take a stroll in the grounds. Quite a

few of them are out there,' replied Sue. 'Mind you, Mr Gill prefers it if first-time guests wait in their room until they've had a visit, either from him or his deputy, Simon Ellis.'

'I see,' said Natalie meekly. As soon as she was alone she started unpacking, then undressed, showered and put on a short-sleeved summer dress. She was just brushing her long blonde hair when the door to her room opened and a tall, dark man entered.

'Hi!' he said. But although his voice was friendly there was no smile on his face. 'You're Natalie Bowen, right?'

'That's right,' said Natalie, with a smile. She held out her hand. 'And you're ...?'

'Simon Ellis, your personal instructor for the weekend. You are on the two-weekend course, aren't you?'

'Yes.'

'That's fine. I wanted to make sure I'd got my facts right before we began.' Taking a notepad out of his jacket pocket he looked around for a pen with which to write.

'Here,' said Natalie. 'Use mine. I was just using it to fill in what I wanted for breakfast on this menu card here.'

'Thank you. Well, Natalie, when did you last have an orgasm?'

She'd been half turned away from him as he spoke, but as she realised what he'd asked her she spun round to look at him, her eyes wide with shock. 'Excuse me?'

He frowned. 'Surely you heard what I said?'

'I thought you asked when did I last have an orgasm.'

'That *was* what I said.'

'I don't see what business it is of yours.'

Simon looked thoughtfully at her. '*Everything* about your sexuality is my business. I'm here to help you change. I can hardly do that if I don't know what you're like at the moment.'

Natalie felt very uncomfortable. 'I suppose not,' she muttered.

'You're not expected to argue with me, you know. The moment you come through the doors of The Haven you are expected to be obedient to our wishes here. Failure to comply with this means that you have to leave. Surely you read our literature? Who was it who recommended you anyway?' He started to look through some notes on a clipboard that he'd brought with him.

'It's all right,' said Natalie hastily. 'I just forgot.'

'I see. Let's hope we don't have any further misunderstandings. Perhaps you'll give me an answer now.'

Natalie was very embarrassed. 'It must have been over two months ago,' she admitted at last.

'Really?' Simon raised his eyebrows. 'You mean you haven't even masturbated in all that time?'

'No.'

'Why not?' His voice was disbelieving.

'Because I haven't had time. I'm so tired when I get home from work that all I want to do is have a glass of wine and go to bed.'

'If sex isn't important to you why are you here?' he asked.

Natalie struggled to explain. She was beginning to feel very uncomfortable as he fired intimate questions at her. 'It is important to me, but I prefer my sex to be with a partner.'

'You can hardly expect good sex with a partner if you don't keep in practice. Right, take off your dress and panties, then sit in that chair over there.'

The palms of Natalie's hands felt damp. Here she was, trapped in a house in the middle of the Sussex countryside with an unknown man ordering her to strip. She could understand why Jan had been hesitant about putting her name forward, because for Natalie the situation was almost unbearable. She swallowed hard. 'Now?'

'Well, I don't intend to go away and come back again when you're ready for me. Come along, Natalie, it's a very simple order.'

Clumsily Natalie did as he'd instructed her, but it was only when she actually sat in the large armchair that she realised it wasn't a normal chair. The seat, which was very deep, sloped sharply backwards and the back was higher than on a normal chair. When she sat down the chair tipped back a little, lifting her feet off the ground.

She watched Simon cross the room towards her. As he drew closer she could see that his dark hair had a few flecks of silver in it, and that despite the darkness of his eyes and eyebrows he had a very pale complexion. His shoulders were broad, his waist slim and he had wonderful cheekbones.

His face would have been attractive but for the fact that there was no warmth, no softness about him. Instead there was a very real suggestion of danger in the set of his mouth, and in the way his eyes flicked over her. Without a word he grasped her ankles and pushed her legs back so that they were hooked over the arms of the chair. 'That's better,' he said, staring down at her.

Natalie began to blush. She was totally open to him, with her entire vulva on view. She desperately wanted to cover herself up, but lacked the courage.

'Right, now masturbate yourself for me,' he said calmly.

It was too much. 'I can't,' she blurted out.

'What do you mean, you can't?'

'I'm sorry but it's too embarrassing. I feel dreadful, sitting here like this with you ...'

He sighed. 'I hope you're not going to be difficult,' he said, with icy politeness. 'Did I not explain to you a few minutes ago that here at The Haven obedience is everything?'

'Yes.'

'You're an intelligent woman, I understand. You run your own business – what is it, now?' His eyes flicked over her notes again. 'Ah yes, you run your own magazine. Well, you should certainly be bright enough to understand what the word "obedience" means, then.'

'Of course I do.'

'Then start obeying me. This is only your initial

assessment: I dread to think what you're going to be like when you start mixing with the other guests. You're certainly going to need a lot of instruction from me, I can see that already.'

Natalie wondered whether this was a good thing or not. She rather suspected that it wasn't. He took two paces back and then waited, with his arms crossed, for her to begin. She wanted to weep with the humiliation of it all. This wasn't what she'd expected, but then Jan hadn't really given her any idea what went on. She'd said that it was against the rules, and Natalie could understand why. Slowly, reluctantly, she allowed her hand to move down over her belly.

'Stop,' said Simon harshly, and her hand froze in mid-movement. 'You don't have to rush things. Caress your breasts first.'

Natalie felt very awkward. 'But that's not how I usually masturbate,' she explained.

'Nevertheless, it's what I want you to do,' he said, clearly exerting iron self-control in order to remain civil. Hastily she moved her right hand upwards and tentatively stroked her left breast. She could tell that he was watching her like a hawk, but despite this, as her fingers lightly touched the delicate skin, she felt her hips twitch slightly and realised that she was becoming excited. Immediately she trailed her fingers down over her ribcage.

'Not yet,' said Simon. '*I'll* tell you when to move your hand.'

Natalie bit her bottom lip, feeling frustrated and resentful, but she did as she was told. For what seemed like endless minutes she continued to caress each of her breasts in turn, until they were hard and aching, the nipples standing out proudly. Only then did Simon allow her to move her hand lower, but even so he insisted that she spent several minutes stroking her belly and outer thighs.

By this time there was a dull ache between her legs and she could feel her sex lips opening up. When Simon finally allowed her to touch herself between her thighs she was shamefully damp and her fingers slid easily up and down the soft channel inside her outer sex lips.

When he didn't give her any further instructions Natalie ran her finger around the entrance to her vagina for a few seconds before drawing it upwards, moving over the moist, silken flesh until she was able to touch the side of her swollen clitoris. Normally it took her a long time to masturbate herself to a climax but this time it was much easier. Already the ache was turning into a pleasurable pulsating sensation. Warmth suffused her lower belly, then her clitoris started to retract as her climax grew nearer.

'Bear down,' said Simon.

Startled by the interruption Natalie lost her rhythm for a moment, and uttered a tiny cry of disappointment as the imminent climax ebbed away. She guessed that if she disobeyed him again she wouldn't be allowed to complete even her first weekend. Knowing that her clitoris, although fully exposed once more, would be too sensitive to touch she could only circle around it, waiting until the delicious tingling began again.

She could hear her breathing growing heavy in the silent room and when she moved her finger in and out of the entrance to her vagina she instinctively tightened herself internally, so that the increased pressure sent sharp spirals of pleasure racing through her lower body.

'Touch your G-spot,' said Simon.

'I've never managed to find it,' gasped the excited Natalie, mortified at her own ignorance.

'Well, that's something we'll get put right over the weekend. Carry on, then.'

She couldn't have stopped even if he'd told her to because now her whole body felt tight, and moving her hand higher she once more rubbed softly against the side of the tight nub, then whimpered with delight as a violent orgasm tore through her.

Natalie's breathing was still rapid and her pulse racing when Simon moved nearer to her. 'Hopefully that's reminded your body of what an orgasm's like. We don't like our clients to begin any sessions cold, as it were.'

'What do you want me to do now?' asked Natalie, breathlessly.

The corners of Simon's mouth turned up slightly. 'That's better – far more the way you're expected to behave here. Since you've asked so nicely you can get up and get dressed.'

She felt a pang of disappointment, having half hoped that there might be more pleasure to come from him. It was mortifying to see how apparently unmoved he was by what he'd been witnessing. But when she took her eyes off his face and glanced lower she could see a tell-tale bulge in the crotch of his trousers, which was quite a relief. A relief, yet also humiliating. Never before had she masturbated herself to orgasm in front of a man, not even to please a lover, let alone a perfect stranger.

As she dressed, Simon glanced at his clipboard. 'Right, there are a few more things I need to know before I leave you. First of all, your favourite sexual position?'

'I'm not sure that you'll approve,' muttered Natalie. She could tell from the expression on his face that he was amused by her reply.

'We don't judge people here. We simply aim to help you change, which is, after all, why you've chosen to visit us. We can hardly help you change if we don't know what you've been doing in the past. I assure you there's nothing personal in this. I neither approve nor disapprove of anything I see or hear when working at The Haven.'

'I prefer to be on top,' she admitted.

'Kneeling on top?'

'Yes.'

'Where you can control all the movement?'

'Of course. That's why I like it.'

'Quite. Have you ever experimented with games of bondage?'

'Certainly not!'

where I'd learn to grow and change sexually. An opportunity for me to experiment, but in a safe environment.'

Simon nodded approvingly. 'That's very well put. You are indeed in a safe environment, very safe. The problem is, you have no experience whatsoever of the kind of things that you're going to be expected to do over the next two weekends. I'll be honest with you, Natalie, I don't believe that you're going to stay the course.'

'What gives you the right to pass judgement on me?' she demanded, furious that anyone should imagine she would quit anything once she'd set her mind to it.

'I'm very good at analysing people's sexual preferences and abilities. You've spent so long in the driving seat I can't imagine you're going to be willing to move over and become a passenger. Still, it's up to you to prove me wrong, isn't it?'

'It certainly is,' she said angrily.

'And that's another thing,' he remarked. 'Your demeanour should be respectful and obedient at all times, even towards me, your personal instructor. I know I've annoyed you, but so will other people during your stay. You have to learn to subdue your natural reactions and accept things with a smile, or even an apology for your own shortcomings.'

Luckily for Natalie, just as she was about to say that Jan hadn't told her any of this and if she'd known she probably wouldn't have come, Simon abruptly left the room.

He'd left a brochure on her dressing table. Opening it up, she read that there was a general meeting in the main reception hall for pre-dinner drinks at seven-thirty. That meant she had another hour and a half to kill and she decided that a walk in the grounds might help her settle down. At the moment both her mind and her body were in turmoil.

Leaving her room, she walked along the corridor. As she passed one of the doors she saw that it was half open and there were strange noises coming from inside. Anxious to know what was happening, she glanced in.

A tall, strongly built man in his mid-thirties was standing in the middle of the room, stark naked. His hands were fastened behind his back and his eyes were blindfolded. Sue, who Natalie had last seen at reception, was kneeling between his legs. Her hands were caressing the man's outer thighs while her mouth and tongue were busily working away, licking and sucking at his testicles and the shaft of his rigid erection. He was trembling from head to foot, the muscles of his abdomen rigid and strange guttural noises, which were what had attracted Natalie's attention, were coming from his mouth.

'Only another five minutes and then you'll be allowed to come,' said Sue, taking her mouth away from him for a moment and giving him a few seconds' respite.

'I can't last that long,' he shouted.

'I'm afraid you have to, otherwise you'll be punished – and I'm sure you remember from your last visit what *that* means.'

Natalie could hardly breathe. She'd never seen anything like this in her life. The veins were bulging on the underside of the man's swollen cock and the tip was an angry purple. Every now and then his hips would jerk forward as some particularly intimate caress of the girl's velvet-soft lips brought him nearer and nearer to the peak of ecstasy. It was easy to see how frantically he was trying to obey the girl's command. But even as Natalie watched, he gave an agonised cry of despair and shuddered violently as he failed, spilling himself into Sue's mouth.

When his body was finally still Sue stood up, and Natalie saw her tweak one of the man's nipples savagely. 'You're a very slow learner, aren't you?' she said calmly. Then she turned to shut the door. Hastily, Natalie hurried on down the corridor, hoping that she hadn't been seen. But what she'd witnessed was etched indelibly on her mind.

As well as frightening her it had left her highly aroused. As Natalie walked through the beautiful grounds all that she could think of was the man's straining erection, heaving chest – and the tight tendons of his neck when he'd thrown his head back in despair as he finally came.

Chapter Four

At seven-thirty precisely, Simon Ellis and the other tutors followed Rob Gill into the reception room, where their twenty weekend guests were waiting for them. As usual on the first evening of a course, the guests were standing awkwardly in small groups, most of them feeling nervous and – probably for the first time in years – unsure of themselves.

It was a moment that Simon always enjoyed. He loved the anxious expressions on the guests' faces as they looked up at the tutors: it gave him a wonderful feeling of power. It was especially good on a day like this, when he'd had such a dreadful week working as a freelance journalist. Out there, in the real world, it was quite different for him than for most of their guests. He was struggling to carve himself a niche, whereas all these people were hugely successful. They were the kind of people who could make or break him, which made his work here all the sweeter.

As Rob started his usual opening speech Simon looked down from the raised dais, letting his eyes wander over the room. He was looking for Natalie Bowen, and it was easy to spot her. She was the tallest woman there, and also the most elegant. Her long wavy blonde hair fell loosely to her shoulders and the simple blue dress that she was wearing accentuated her slender figure. He could picture her long slim legs beneath it very clearly. Even while he'd been assessing her in a professional manner, another part of his mind had appreciated those legs. They were unusually good and he was looking forward to initiating her into the ways of The Haven.

Feeling his manhood stir, he tried to distract himself by looking at some of the other people. It was unusual for him to be this excited by someone so early on. Of course, during therapy sessions he always became highly aroused – he had to or he wouldn't have been able to do his job – but this seemed more personal. He wondered if it had something to do with the fact that Natalie was in the same line of business as him, only far more successful. Whatever the reason, it was going to add an extra dimension of pleasure to the weekend.

Realising that Rob's speech was drawing to a close, Simon looked at the sheet of paper in his hand. On it were three names: two women's and a man's. Naturally, Natalie was one of the women. Over the next two days she would do nothing without him either participating or being there to watch her progress. They had several other tutors, but Simon was second only to Rob. He was usually assigned to the people who Rob reckoned were going to have the most trouble. In the case of Natalie Bowen, Simon was certain that his boss was right.

'That's all I have to say,' concluded Rob. Then he turned to the assorted male and female tutors standing on the platform behind him. Only Simon was allowed to stand next to him, as a sign to the guests that he was second in the chain of command.

'The tutors will now let you know what groups you'll be in this evening,' explained Rob. 'After you've eaten, you'll go off in your various groups and your weekend of instruction will begin. I really do hope that come Sunday evening, when we meet in here again, you'll feel that we've more than fulfilled our promise to you all.'

Simon decided that he'd collect his other pupils before Natalie. The man was called Chris, a thirty-year-old commodities broker on his second weekend at The Haven. The other woman was Heather Lacey, at twenty-nine well on her way to becoming a million-airess, thanks to her chain of beauty salons. Like Natalie, this was her first visit, but Simon suspected that she'd be easier to train. She'd seemed almost timid at their initial meeting, although she claimed that she was too forceful for most men.

As Simon, Chris and Heather approached Natalie he saw the blonde's dark blue eyes widen a little, a sure sign that she was feeling very nervous.

The four of them ate together at a secluded corner table, but as usual Simon made sure that the conversation didn't touch on sex. Unlike some of the other instructors he preferred it this way because it kept the clients on edge. He knew that they were expecting some kind of verbal tuition or explanation at this stage. Without it they became confused and thus, in his experience, easier to control later on.

It was gone ten before he finally rose from the table. 'Time to go upstairs,' he explained and then strode swiftly away, leaving his three pupils to hurry after him. He led them up two flights of stairs to the training floor, where each tutor had his own room. Simon's was large, plushly carpeted, with heavy curtains that were tied back at the moment, a big bed, a couch, chairs and several other pieces of equipment that he usually had to use at some stage during every weekend.

Although the decor of the room was attractive there was something forbidding about it, partly because of the subdued lighting. There was no central light, only wall lights. Again, this was part of Simon's strategy for disorientating the visitors. If they were too relaxed, too at ease, it was difficult to 'persuade' them to change their ways, even though that was what they were paying for.

He looked at Chris. 'Take your clothes off,' he ordered him. Chris, having already spent one weekend at The Haven, obeyed immediately. Simon noticed that Heather and Natalie had moved closer together and were watching nervously.

Chris was a fairly short man, but one of his hobbies was working out with his private trainer and as a result he had an excellent physique. He also had an enormous cock. At the moment it was lying limply against his left thigh, but Simon knew it would soon start to move. He remembered Chris as being far too quick off the mark, one of the things that he was having to learn to control. One of the reasons that he'd come to them was that his own pleasure came first for him, and he was finding it hard to subdue his natural responses in order to give his partner more pleasure.

'Right, girls, strip down to your underwear,' said Simon. They both hesitated, glancing awkwardly at each other. 'It's an order, not a request,' he reminded them. 'If either of you is too slow, I shall have to chastise you.' Immediately the two women began to take off their dresses.

Simon caught hold of Heather's hand. She was only wearing a chemise and French knickers, and her full breasts made an immediate impression on Chris whose penis began to stir.

'Use your mouth on him until he's hard,' said Simon, seeing from his notes on Heather that she didn't like performing fellatio on her partners.

Heather looked at him in horror. 'I don't even know him. That's not something that I do—'

'Which is precisely why you're here. You do *want* to change, don't you, Heather?'

'Yes, but—'

'There is no "but" about it. Don't keep him waiting any longer: he's getting excited enough without you touching him.'

As Heather slowly dropped to her knees and began tentatively to lick the head of Chris's rapidly hardening cock, Simon looked at Natalie. She was wearing a lacy bra and high-cut bikini pants, her long legs encased in silky hold-up stockings. She was, Simon realised, his idea of the perfect woman: he'd always had a weakness for tall, slim blondes. He knew that he mustn't let her discover this, or Rob either. Any kind of emotional involvement between tutors and clients was strictly forbidden at The Haven.

'While Heather's doing that you can stand behind Chris and rub yourself against him,' he said firmly. Natalie didn't attempt to argue. Soon she was pressing herself against Chris's buttocks and back, her slim hips moving gently from side to side and her lace-encased breasts caressing the flesh of his back.

As Chris grew larger and harder so Heather grew visibly more reluctant, more unwilling. Despite what she'd been told, she kept taking breaks, moving her head away and glancing up at Simon as she waited to be allowed to finish. Simon ignored the mute appeal in her pleading eyes. 'Remember, Chris, you're not to come,' he cautioned the hapless young man as he was tormented almost to distraction by the two lovely women.

'For God's sake, don't make me wait too long,' gasped Chris. 'This is worse than last weekend.'

'Of course it is – you're not a novice any more. Heather, you carry on, you're doing very well. Natalie, I want you over here in the middle of the bed.' Catching hold of her hand Simon drew her across the room, got her to remove her underwear, then positioned her on all fours. There was a sheen of perspiration down her spine and he smiled inwardly. Clearly, despite her reservations, she was already turned on.

'Don't move,' he told her. 'You're to wait like that until I let Chris take you. When he does, it's not going to be long before he climaxes. It's up to you to climax before him.'

Natalie looked at him as though he was mad. 'I'll never be able to come like that, not if he just takes me, particularly in this position.'

'In that case, I'm afraid you'll have to be punished

when he's finished. Think about that while you're waiting.' There was a sudden moan from Chris and Simon hastily left Natalie on her hands and knees in the middle of the bed and went to check on Chris's progress.

Natalie waited, trembling, on the bed. She wished with all her heart that she hadn't come on this weekend. Never, not in her wildest dreams, had she envisaged a scene like this. The fact that she was about to let a stranger penetrate her, take her in a way that she didn't even find exciting, and have two other people watching her while he did it was horrifying. The strange thing was that although the situation horrified her, it also excited her. All her nerve endings seemed to be jangling in expectation. When she'd been rubbing herself against Chris she'd nearly come simply by pressing her pubic mound against him and imagining what it must feel like for him having to subdue his own excitement.

Now, though, she had something to worry about. Despite the fact that her body was aroused she knew from past experience that she wasn't going to come when Chris took her from behind. Which meant that she was going to have to endure being punished by Simon, something that filled her with dread.

Behind her Natalie heard Heather being told to stop. Then, a few seconds later, the bed moved as Chris scrambled on to it. 'Lower your arms and rest your forehead on the mattress,' suggested Simon. 'That way you're more open for him.' She'd hardly had time to obey before she felt Chris's hands gripping her round the waist. Then, with one quick thrust, he was deep inside her, his enormous erection stretching her so much that it was almost painful.

'Slow down, Chris,' said Simon. 'Remember, Natalie has to try and have an orgasm before you.'

'I've already had to wait,' complained Chris. 'I'm sorry, but I can't hold back much longer.'

In a despairing attempt to trigger an orgasm for herself Natalie started to clench and release her internal muscles, contracting them around the massive girth of Chris's cock. It worked, because tiny darts of pleasure began to move through her. But then, before they had a chance to grow into anything more, Chris's hips moved faster and faster, his hips slammed against her buttocks and within a few seconds he uttered a cry of triumph as his pleasure peaked.

'You didn't come, Natalie, did you?' demanded Simon. She could have wept with a mixture of fear and frustration. Despite the fact that she thought everything had been wrong for her, she'd come so close to an orgasm. 'Chris was too quick,' she complained.

'No, *you* were too *slow*,' retorted Simon. 'Right, Chris, I want you to use your mouth on Heather now. It's her turn for some pleasure. Natalie, come and stand over here by me. You'll be punished after the other two have gone.'

Nervously, Natalie scrambled off the bed and then stood next to Simon, watching as the reluctant Heather lay on her back in the middle of the bed. Chris tried to put his head between her thighs, but she was squeezing them too tightly together. Simon frowned. 'This won't do. Natalie, you and I will have to help Chris. We'll each take hold of one of Heather's ankles and spread her legs further apart.'

'Please don't!' cried Heather.

Simon ignored her. Natalie caught hold of one of Heather's ankles, pulling it towards the bottom left-hand corner of the bed, whilst Simon tugged her other leg in the opposite direction. Now Chris had free access to Heather, access that was made even easier for him when Simon wrenched her French knickers down roughly and pushed a pillow beneath her hips.

Natalie felt Heather's body stiffen in resistance as Chris started to lick and suck between her thighs. 'He's doing it too hard,' Heather protested.

'Yes, we're working on that,' said Simon. 'Be careful, Chris. I'm sure you don't want to be punished, especially when you've done so well up to now.'

Chris seemed to take the hint because gradually Heather's taut body relaxed, although it was obvious that she was finding it hard to get any pleasure from what was being done to her. 'Curl your tongue inside her,' suggested Simon helpfully. 'See if you can find her G-spot and flick at that.' All at once Natalie felt the muscles in Heather's leg go rigid, and her head began moving restlessly from side to side as tiny whimpers of excitement escaped from her. Then, with startling speed, she was shaken by a violent tremor.

'There,' said Simon in a satisfied voice. 'That wasn't so bad, was it? Well done, Chris. You've excelled yourself this evening. You and Heather can both go to your rooms now.'

Natalie looked anxiously at him. 'What about me?'

'You know very well that you can't go. *You* have to be punished.'

Heather grabbed her clothes, gave Natalie a

sympathetic look and fled from the room, clearly embarrassed by what had happened to her but still flushed with the pleasure she'd been given. Chris was far more relaxed about it all and looked pleased with himself, although he too gave Natalie a pitying glance. 'What are you going to do?' she asked nervously.

'You'll find out in a minute. See that stool over there?' She nodded. 'I want you to bend over that. Keep your feet on the ground but make sure that your breasts are hanging down. As you're tall, you shouldn't have any problem.'

Natalie began to tremble. 'I want to know what you're going to do to me.'

'As I said, you'll find out in a moment. You don't like taking orders, do you?'

'Not if I'm going to be hurt.'

'I don't think you like taking them at all,' said Simon sharply.

'What's that to you?' asked Natalie, in astonishment.

He realised that the remark had been unprofessional and quickly tried to cover his mistake. 'Nothing. Only from a tutor's viewpoint.'

Natalie didn't believe him. She had a feeling that it was more personal than that, but she couldn't prove it.

In any case, she was as interested in Simon as he appeared to be in her. He seemed detached and dangerous, yet she felt certain that he could, if he wanted, be an incredibly good lover.

'Hurry up!' he said, breaking into her reverie. 'You have to obey commands quicker than this, I'm afraid, otherwise you've wasted your money.'

Unable to put off the moment any longer, Natalie bent over the tall stool, feeling the blood rush to her breasts as they dangled down. She wanted to lift her head and glance over her shoulder to see what was about to happen but she'd already learned better. She waited tensely and then she felt Simon's hand moving softly over her body.

He was spreading some kind of oil over her. It felt delicious and, as he rubbed it over her lower back and into the tiny dent at the base of her spine, she gave a small sigh of pleasure. Surely this couldn't be her punishment, she thought, because if so she wouldn't mind how many times she was punished. He continued to massage the oil into her buttocks and back for several minutes before moving away for a few seconds.

When he returned Natalie's body was soft and receptive – she was almost drifting off to sleep. Then, with no warning at all, she felt a sharp stinging pain on her buttocks and gave a cry of astonishment.

'That hurt.'

'It was meant to hurt. You're being punished, remember. It's only a latex crop. You won't be marked or damaged in any way,' said Simon. For the first time his voice was gentle, soothing. 'Stay relaxed, Natalie. If you go with this, you'll find that there can be pleasure in it, too.'

Natalie didn't believe him for a minute. She was horrified. Never in her life had anyone ever struck her during sex. But before she could say any more the latex crop had fallen on her oiled flesh again and once more the hot, stinging sensation coursed through her. Only this time the pain wasn't as great. She relaxed a little and when Simon struck her for the third time she realised that he was right. Her skin was starting to feel pleasurably warm, the stinging was more of an irritation than a pain and there was an insistent throbbing starting between her thighs. She could feel her clitoris hardening, too, and she began to wriggle against the stool, straining to stimulate herself a little.

'That's not allowed,' said Simon. But he didn't sound angry, he sounded amused. 'You see, I was right about the punishment, wasn't I?' He struck her twice more until all her lower torso felt as though it was on fire. Despite his remonstration she started to writhe against the stool again, frantic to bring about the pleasurable climax that she knew was so close.

'Keep *still* when you're told,' said Simon, his voice harsher this time and, with a groan, she obeyed him. Then, to her relief, she felt his hand slide beneath her: now his knowing fingers were parting her sex lips, pressing up against her vulva and probing relentlessly for the tiny, hard little nub that was desperate to be touched.

The moment Simon's oiled fingers found her clitoris Natalie moaned with relief. He moved his fingers so skilfully, touching her exactly as she liked to be touched, that within a few brief seconds her muscles slithered, coiled and gathered themselves together in a tight knot before dissolving into a blissfully intense orgasm that flooded through every inch of her.

'I'm not sure whether that will teach you to obey me in the future or not,' said Simon dryly. 'You'd better get dressed and go back to your room now. Tomorrow will be a very busy day for you.'

Chapter Five

Next morning Natalie opened her eyes to find Simon standing over her. 'Is something the matter?' she asked.

'It's seven o'clock. Time for your day to begin.'

She was still half asleep, and rather confused. 'What do you mean?'

'I mean that we start early here, to make sure you get full value for money. Incidentally, I don't believe that you've met Marc. He's a trainee tutor, and he'll be observing what we do over the next two days. From time to time he may also take part. You'd better put on a robe: we're going to my room again.'

'I can't go before I've showered,' protested Natalie.

'Of course you can. This is an example of impulsive sex.'

'I don't like impulsive sex. I like to have a shower first, make myself nice and—'

'But that's what we're trying to change, isn't it, Natalie?' Simon said softly. 'You're much too fussy for your own good. Now, if I were your lover, rather than your tutor, I'd be very disappointed at your reaction this morning. Personally, I enjoy a lazy early-morning session in bed.'

Realising that she had no choice but to obey, Natalie grabbed her cotton robe. Then, with her feet bare and her blonde hair still tousled from a night's sleep, she followed the two men up to the top floor of The Haven.

Walking into Simon's instruction room she saw that Heather had already been fetched and was perched on the edge of one of the chairs, looking extremely disgruntled. Clearly, she was no keener than Natalie on being woken this early for sex. Her short light brown hair was unbrushed and her eyelids were heavy, as though she hadn't had enough sleep that night.

'Right: our aim this morning is an orgasm before

breakfast,' explained Simon. 'I can tell that neither of you two are particularly keen on the idea, but I assure you that in the future your lovers will appreciate it. The problem with both of you is that you only want sex when and where you choose. There doesn't seem to be much give-and-take in your lives. You both feel the need to stay in control at all times. Well, right now that control's been taken away from you. I really hope that you'll both come to understand how much more exciting life can be if you allow that to happen.'

He glanced at the pair of them, then smiled at Natalie. It wasn't a friendly smile, more an amused one. 'We'll start with you. Marc, have you put the bolster on the bed?' Marc nodded. 'Good. Then take your clothes off and lie on your back on that, Natalie.'

Natalie's heart sank. Clearly she was going to be expected to have sex in the missionary position, her least favourite – which probably meant yet another frustrating session followed by some kind of punishment. She felt extremely resentful as she dropped her clothes on the floor and got on to the bed.

Taking off his own clothes, Simon lay down next to

her. 'You don't look very relaxed, nor, I'm sorry to say, at all sexy.'

'That's probably because I don't *feel* relaxed or sexy.'

'You know, you're not trying very hard to change, are you?' he whispered softly. Then he grasped her chin tightly with his fingers. 'I hope you're not going to be too difficult. It will be such a waste of your money – and of my time. There's a long list of people waiting to come to The Haven. You're taking up a place for two whole weekends. The least you can do is try and get maximum benefit from your stay.'

'I didn't know it would be like this,' Natalie hissed, her temper getting the better of her. 'I thought there'd be more lectures and group discussions. Jan didn't tell me what was going to happen.'

'If you don't like it, you can always go home.'

'You'd like that, wouldn't you?' muttered Natalie. 'You told me yesterday that you didn't think I'd stay the course, and I can tell you want to prove you're right. I don't know why, but I get the feeling you don't like me one little bit.'

'You're quite wrong,' Simon said softly. 'I like you a lot, rather too much, in fact, but I *don't* like your kind of sexuality in a woman.'

'I didn't think you were meant to feel things personally,' said Natalie. She felt a sense of triumph at having forced an admission of involvement from this remote, dark stranger who held such a peculiar fascination for her.

'I'm not. Now, could we get on with the lesson, please? You told me when I was filling in your admission form that you always preferred to be on top during sex. I'm now going to attempt to teach you that it can be equally pleasurable when you're not. Heather has the same problem, so I want her to watch what we do very carefully'

As Simon spoke he started to run his hands over Natalie's body, tracing circles around each of her small but firm breasts, pausing occasionally to tease the tips of the nipples, rolling them between his finger and thumb.

It felt delicious and Natalie started to relax, although she knew that it was a waste of time getting excited. She'd never yet managed to climax in this position. Simon's hands moved on down over her ribcage and across her stomach. Then he lowered his head and swirled his tongue in her belly button, which made her stomach jerk. He spent a long time caressing her belly, hips and outer thighs and while he was stroking her there she felt someone licking and nibbling at her toes. Startled, she raised her head and saw that it was Marc.

'Lie back and enjoy the sensations,' said Simon. 'Marc knows what he's doing. He was well instructed by me before we collected you.'

Natalie was becoming very excited. There was something deliciously decadent about having two men concentrating on giving her pleasure. Her toes curled as Marc's tongue ran along the tendons of her high instep. When he nibbled on the tight flesh around her ankle bone she shivered with delight. All the while Simon's hands continued to caress her lower body, but they never strayed between her thighs.

Finally Marc removed his mouth from Natalie's feet and now Simon positioned himself above her, his dark eyes staring down into hers. 'You know you could have a climax if you wanted to, don't you?' he said quietly. 'You're aroused enough.' Reaching between her thighs he ran his fingers over the tell-tale dampness of her vulva.

'I want to come,' she cried. 'But I know I won't.'

'Of course you will.' He began to lower himself on to her, but only the bottom half of his body rested against her because he kept himself supported on his arms, lifting his chest away from her. For the first time she felt his penis touching her, nudging between her outer sex lips and then moving up and down the slick channel as her body opened to welcome him.

To Natalie's delight Simon didn't enter her at once. Instead, he moved his hips around, pressing against her pubic mound and sliding the soft tip of his erection over her clitoris. Unlike most men, he'd positioned himself with his legs outside hers, which meant that there was more pressure on her vulva: her nerve ends reacted immediately. She felt tendrils of pleasure spreading slowly through her body, moving upwards from between her thighs all the way to the small swollen globes of her breasts.

Natalie could feel that she was near to climaxing, that if she could only give herself over to what was happening, allow herself to receive the pleasure that Simon was giving her and completely relax then she would come. But it was impossible. No matter how skilfully he moved, or how slowly he slid inside her, rotating his hips in a circular motion before withdrawing and sliding up to touch her clitoris once more, the final moment of release refused to come.

Her body was so tight that she felt she'd explode if she didn't climax. But she longed to roll Simon over, to sit astride him, moving herself up and down on his wonderful erection, bending forward so that he could suck on her aching nipples as she came. It was all she could picture, and the more she thought about that, the quicker the delicious sensations that Simon had brought about faded.

Frantic for satisfaction, Natalie jerked her hips upwards, trying to control the pace as her hands gripped Simon's buttocks in an attempt to alter his rhythm. Immediately Simon's body froze.

'Now you've spoilt it, haven't you?' he said.

Left stranded, her nerve endings still jangling and the sensations slowly dissipating, she looked miserably at him. 'What do you mean?'

'You tried to take control again.'

'I couldn't help it. You weren't doing it right, you—'

'And I thought you were doing so well,' Simon said sadly as he lifted his body off hers.

'Don't leave me like this!' she cried.

'I'm sorry, but you have to learn. I warned you that you were going to find it difficult. Let's see if Heather has better luck than you.'

'Can't we try again?' asked Natalie. She knew that if she could only have one more try, if she closed her eyes and allowed him to do what he wanted, then the pleasure would come again. She was frantic to feel the glorious excitement once more.

'You only get one turn,' Simon said curtly. Then, catching hold of her hand, he pulled her off the bed. 'Put your nightdress and robe back on, and see if you can learn by watching Heather.'

'I don't *want* to watch Heather,' she muttered.

'Then you should have done as you were told, shouldn't you? Come along, Heather. Do you think you can do better than Natalie?'

Heather didn't answer. She was clearly turned on by what she'd been watching, and for a moment Natalie hated her. If she'd gone second, then she'd probably have done better. It was unfair of Simon to make her have the first turn, and she knew that he'd done it on purpose to make it more difficult for her.

As Heather climbed on to the bolster, and Simon began to caress her slightly larger breasts, Natalie remembered how it had felt when he'd touched her. She shivered. Her whole body was becoming aroused again, and there was nothing she could do about it. She was going to have to watch while Heather received all the pleasuring that she, Natalie, had so foolishly thrown away.

Simon did all the things to Heather that he'd done to Natalie. As far as Natalie could tell there was no difference at all in his approach, and this upset her because while he'd been touching her it had seemed personal. She'd believed that he felt something for her. Watching him now, she saw that she'd been wrong. It was as he'd said: he was simply doing his job – and, by the sound of the noises that Heather was making, doing it very well.

When Marc started licking between Heather's toes the other woman became frantic with excitement, allowing the pleasure to swamp her and not resisting it as Natalie had done. When Marc had finished and stood back from the bed, Heather did attempt to wriggle free as Simon placed his body on top of hers. But the brief moment of resistance quickly passed once she felt him pressing against her pubic mound. Soon Natalie saw the pink flush of arousal spreading over Heather's chest and neck.

She could imagine only too well the pressure that was building inside the other woman. The wonderful tightening of her muscles, the piercing shards of pleasure that were almost certainly shooting through her lower belly as Simon moved up and down her soft, moist flesh before sliding into her welcoming entrance.

Unlike Natalie, Heather was moaning aloud with excitement and she made no attempt to control Simon in any way. In fact, she seemed to be lost in her own world, a world made up entirely of sensations, sensations that Natalie, standing helplessly as she watched, could only remember and regret. It quickly became obvious that, unlike Natalie, Heather was going to climax. Natalie, who had never before watched a couple having sex like this, wondered if she was going to come as well. She felt ready to, but her body needed a caress, an intimate touch and she knew that Marc wouldn't be allowed to touch her.

After several minutes, Simon's pace quickened, but he was still well in control of himself. The same couldn't be said for Heather, whose breathing was loud and rapid. Then, with a keening cry, she came. Natalie watched as Heather's body twisted and turned beneath Simon's lean hardness until suddenly the other woman's eyes closed and she lay still and relaxed, her body limp.

'Was that the first time you've ever come when you were underneath a man?' Simon asked dispassionately. His clipped voice shattered the erotically charged atmosphere in the room.

'Yes,' admitted Heather.

'You did very well. We'll be able to try you with someone else later this morning.' He glanced at his watch. 'Time for you both to get ready for breakfast. At half-past ten I'm taking you to watch the men learning to be submissive. *You* should enjoy that,' he added, looking directly at Natalie.

I don't like submissive men,' she said defensively.

'Really? Then what sort of men *do* you like? Dominant males don't take very kindly to being told what to do.'

'That's probably why I'm so unsuccessful in my relationships.'

'Precisely,' he said softly. 'Which is why I want to help you learn to change. The trouble is, you don't really want to be helped.'

Natalie wanted to tell Simon that he was wrong, that she *did* want to change but it was hard to give up control. However, she didn't have a chance because, before she could reply, he and Marc had walked out of the room, leaving her and Heather alone together.

Heather looked at Natalie. 'It's rather embarrassing, all this, isn't it?'

'It's not at all what I expected,' admitted Natalie. 'I hadn't thought there would be so much ... practical work, as it were.'

'I had no idea what to expect, but I didn't really care,' confessed Heather. 'I was so tired of losing men whom I really liked that I was willing to do anything if it was going to make me happier.'

'But *will* this make us happier?' asked Natalie. 'How do we know it's what *we* really want, rather than what men want us to be?'

'That bothered me a bit. But after this morning I'm beginning to see the advantages,' said Heather, with a laugh. 'He's absolutely incredible, isn't he?'

'Who?'

'Simon, of course.'

'He's all right.'

'Oh come on, he knows all the right buttons to push.'

'Of course he does, that's his job. It doesn't mean he's a particularly nice person, or even a particularly sexy one. I think you must have to be a bit strange to be able to do the kind of work he does.'

'I should think most men would give their eye-teeth for a job like that,' remarked Heather. 'I certainly don't think he's strange. I just wish that we were allowed to fraternise with the tutors after we leave here. If I'm going to start a new way of life, I'd like him to join in the fun. He'd be a great party guest.'

'Did you find it easy to have an orgasm?' asked Natalie, hesitantly. 'I thought it was really difficult. I never like being underneath, but having people watching, and knowing that Simon was assessing me, made it even worse. I nearly managed it, but he wasn't moving quite how I wanted him to.'

'It was probably easier for me,' admitted Heather. 'After all, I'd watched the pair of you and, believe me, that was an incredible turn-on. That's another thing: I could never have imagined myself watching people having sex before this weekend. Actually, I thought he did everything right. You probably wanted to guide him just to show that he wasn't having things all his own way.'

'What are you, some kind of amateur psychiatrist?' asked Natalie, beginning to get irritated.

'Sorry, I didn't mean to upset you. It's just that I know how difficult it is, and I thought that we should try and help each other.'

Natalie felt ashamed of herself. 'You're right, we should help each other. Probably I was too busy worrying that my pleasure was totally in his hands. But it's a difficult habit to break.'

'What do you think about watching men being forced to be submissive, then?'

Natalie thought for a moment. 'I can't really picture it, can you?'

'No, but it should be very interesting. The men here are all like us, very successful in their particular line of business. I was talking to one in the grounds yesterday when I arrived. He's head of a big multinational company and when he says "Jump" everyone jumps. He's been married twice and had three other failed relationships. He says that he can't modify his behaviour at all, that he finds himself taking over in bed even when he knows that's not what the woman wants. I'd quite like to watch him being tutored. He was very attractive.'

'He was probably attractive to you because he is powerful and important,' pointed out Natalie. 'He won't be nearly as attractive if he's seen being submissive.'

'It's odd, isn't it?' said Heather. 'We both like being in control in bed, but neither of us are attracted to submissive men. No wonder we were making such a mess of our private lives.'

Natalie glanced at the clock on the wall. 'We'd better go and get ready for breakfast. I think they stop serving at nine.'

'Yes, better not be late or no doubt that will be considered a punishable offence as well.'

Natalie looked thoughtfully at the other woman. 'You know, I think you're going to learn to change quicker than I am.'

'Why do you say that?'

'I don't know. Perhaps it's because you're more relaxed about the whole thing than I am. Anyway, seeing you with Simon just now it was obvious that you were able to relinquish control to him.'

'That's not to say I'll be able to relinquish control to someone else.'

Natalie sighed. 'I know. But I haven't managed to relinquish it at all yet.'

Heather smiled reassuringly at her. 'Don't worry, it's

early days and I heard that Simon's never had a failure.'

Natalie shivered. 'He's not going to be very pleased if I'm his first, then, is he?'

'No,' agreed Heather. 'He certainly isn't.'

Chapter Six

At ten-thirty, over an hour after they'd breakfasted, Simon came and collected Natalie and Heather from the lounge, where they'd been chatting together and surreptitiously eyeing the other guests. 'Time for the next part of the learning curve, girls,' he said. 'I expect you've been looking forward to this.'

'Not particularly,' said Natalie. 'I don't think it's going to turn me on.'

Simon looked sceptical. 'How about you, Heather?'

'I'm not sure,' confessed the other woman.

'At least you're open-minded about it. The trouble with you, Natalie, is that you're resisting change every step of the way. You don't seem to realise that you're the only one who's going to lose out. It doesn't matter to me whether you gain anything from your weekends here or not.'

'Really?' asked Natalie. 'I'd have thought it would matter quite a lot to you. After all, you're famous for never having failed.'

'There's no question of passing or failing,' he said sharply. 'This isn't an exam, it's a self-improvement course. You came here because you wanted to change yourself, and if you leave without doing that, then that's your personal choice.'

'So you wouldn't consider it a failure on your part?'

Simon moved closer to her. 'If you're trying to annoy me, don't,' he whispered. 'It's a very dangerous game to play.'

'Perhaps I'm getting a taste for dangerous games.'

'You're not ready to take me on yet,' he said softly. 'You'd be playing out of your league.'

'Are we going or not?' asked Heather.

Simon nodded. 'Yes, we'd better hurry or they'll have started without us. It isn't likely, though: Rob prefers the men to have spectators for this particular exercise.'

The room to which Simon took them both was on

the ground floor. It was large and, again, plushly carpeted, with three old-fashioned *chaise-longues*, but little else in the way of furniture. Rob, his piercing blue eyes bright, was standing at the side of the room with three girls next to him. In the middle of the room there were three men, all of them completely naked.

'Are the women tutors?' Natalie asked Simon.

'No,' he said quietly. 'We don't employ enough staff for all the activities that we run here. Fortunately most of us have friends, broad-minded ones, naturally, who are more than willing to help Rob out. These three are friends of Marc's. They take great pleasure in their work here.'

'What's going to happen?' asked Heather.

Rob glanced over at them. 'Would you all sit down on the floor by the door, please? And I'd be grateful if you didn't chatter while we're working. I know that Andrew, Oliver and Sebastian will appreciate having an audience, but I'd rather it was a silent one.'

'That's told us,' muttered Natalie. Rob gave her a sharp warning glance before turning his attention back to the men, still standing naked in the middle of the room. 'I'd like you to introduce yourselves now,' he ordered them.

The first one stepped forward. Natalie thought that he was probably about forty. He was of average height, with dark brown hair and designer stubble. He looked a typical macho man, and she could imagine the way he'd behave at parties, grasping women's elbows, certain they'd be very grateful to receive his manly attentions. 'I'm Andrew,' he said, his voice aggressive. 'I'm managing director for a sales-and-marketing company and the only thing I really dislike is being called Andy.'

The second man stepped forward. He was an entirely different type. Tall, probably a little over six foot, he was quite slim but raw-boned and his light brown hair was tousled and curly, swept back off his face. He looked to be in his mid-thirties and what made him stand out were his large brown eyes, which were quite soft-looking and fringed with extraordinarily long, thick lashes. 'I'm Oliver, I run my own distribution company and there's nothing I particularly dislike, except women who try to take control in bed.'

'By that I take it that you think you always know best,' commented Rob.

Oliver seemed surprised by the question. 'I think I know how to please a woman.'

'You don't think that women might know their own bodies better than you do?'

Oliver smiled. It was a charming smile. 'They might *think* that they do. But I know that if they gave me a chance to show them what I could do, they'd change their minds.'

'I can understand why you're here, then,' remarked Rob. 'Next.'

The third man stepped forward. He was about the same age and height as Oliver, but more heavily built. 'My name's Sebastian. I'm a company director in the City and I'm here because women tell me I'm too aggressive in bed.'

'Do you think they've got a fair point?' asked Rob, with interest.

'Not really, no. I think most women would like to turn the clock back, but they think it's politically incorrect so they make token objections.'

'I see. You think they'd like to return to the caveman days, do you?'

'Not exactly,' protested Sebastian. 'I'm not suggesting I should hit them over the head and drag them back to my cave. It's just that men are meant to dominate. That's what nature intended.'

'Fine,' said Rob pleasantly. 'Well, now, all three of you have chosen to come on this course because, however strongly you believe your approach to women is right, experience has shown you that you're not forming successful relationships because of a perceived "failure" on your part by the women. You've chosen to come here and learn to change. This is the first visit for all of you, and no doubt already you're finding it rather strange. However, this is the most intensive of your lessons so far and I shall be interested to see how you respond.

'I think it says something about our society today that all of you have positions of power in your work, and so – like many of the women on our course – you continue to use the same attitudes that you use at work when you climb into bed with a partner. What you have to realise is that you don't have to be in control all the time.'

'I'm beginning to think it was a mistake to come on this course,' said Sebastian.

Rob looked questioningly at him. 'Why?'

'Because there are an awful lot of high-flying women who are here learning exactly the same as us. We're all going to end up submissive, and then no one will get any satisfaction.'

'Being less aggressive doesn't necessarily mean being submissive,' said Rob. 'That's something else that I hope you'll come to learn. Now, it's time to begin. Are you ready, girls?' He looked at the three young women standing at his side.

The girls were all very attractive, two of them blondes and one a brunette. Swiftly, they unbuttoned their white overalls and then walked slowly to stand one in front of each of the men. They were all wearing high-heeled shoes and stockings, with short chemises over their bras and panties. Their lingerie was of the same design except one of the blondes' garments was cream-coloured, the other's was black, and the brunette was wearing virginal white.

The girls positioned themselves in front but slightly to the side of the men, which meant that Natalie and the other spectators could watch the men's reactions to what was happening. Slowly, languorously, each of the girls began to strip. Even Natalie could appreciate how arousing the strip was, as they pushed the straps of their chemises down over their shoulders before allowing them to slither down, the silk material caressing their bodies. Then they stepped out of them, still wearing their high heels.

For a few seconds they stood posing provocatively for the men, whose cocks immediately started to harden, and then they started to rub their hands seductively up and down their thighs, letting the fingers slide beneath their stocking tops. As they did this they also rubbed softly at their bellies, just above the line of their panties.

Next they removed their high-cut briefs before lazily unfastening a stocking and slowly rolling it down their long, slender legs. As they bent over, their underwired bras emphasised their cleavages, and Natalie heard all the men draw in their breath together as the women twisted and turned, making sure that their partners could relish every tantalising glimpse of flesh.

Cleverly, despite the fact that they were clearly used to doing this, all the girls pretended to be modest and kept looking downwards. One of the blondes had her face half turned away from Oliver, as though too shy to look at him, and Natalie could see that this was heightening his excitement. His erection looked rock hard, and of the three men he was visibly the most aroused.

The girls left their bras on until last, as though reluctant to display their breasts, and the blonde girl opposite Oliver took longer than the other two about each movement. Twice she reached behind her back and then, as though changing her mind, ran a hand through her hair while her other hand strayed down the side of her body. By this time her left shoulder strap was falling down her arm, but still she kept Oliver waiting and it wasn't until both the other girls were completely naked that she finally seemed to find the courage to unfasten the bra and remove it.

Natalie could tell by the sound of Simon's breathing that even he wasn't impervious to what was going on. Obviously he must have seen it several times before, but for the first time she realised what power women had over men if they pretended to be submissive, even though the men knew that it wasn't true. She wondered what it would feel like to strip for a man in that way, and decided that some time in the future she'd give it a try.

Once naked, the women turned and looked at Rob as he spoke. 'Now then, I want each of you to give your lovely partner an orgasm. However, this can't involve any form of penetration. In other words, you can use your hands, your tongue, or even your toes if you like, but nothing else. There are three *chaise-longues* there, you can go and lie on those whenever you want, but you may well decide to start right where you are. It's entirely up to you. I shall be watching carefully, and shall correct you if I think you're going wrong. Do you understand?'

The three men mumbled an unintelligible response that Natalie assumed to be 'Yes', and then they all stepped forward, anxious to get their hands on the girls.

Natalie wasn't in the least surprised to see that all three men grabbed for the girls' breasts, although Oliver's touch was far more subtle than that of his companions. 'You're not kneading dough, Andrew,' called Rob sharply, and Natalie saw a look of anger cross Andrew's face before he changed the way he was touching the brunette's bust.

Watching the men fondling the girls, she was reminded of the way she'd been handled by many of her lovers. All three of them lacked the subtlety and delicacy that were needed to help women achieve genuine satisfaction. If ever there was anything designed to show why women had started trying to take control in bed, this exhibition was it, she thought to herself. However, she supposed that it was encouraging that some men were beginning to understand that they were going wrong, even if they'd chosen to pay to learn to do it right rather than listen to their partners.

After a few minutes all three of the men either led or carried their partners to the *chaise-longues*. Now Rob allowed the spectators to move forward to the middle of the room, where they had a very good view of what was going on.

It soon became apparent to Natalie that neither Andrew nor Sebastian was taking any notice of his girl's response. However, Oliver was different. Although he was clearly very excited, he still spent time caressing his partner's body, and his mouth travelled from one nipple to the other until the blonde beneath him began to moan softly with rising excitement.

'I really fancy him,' Heather whispered to Natalie. But before she could say more Simon silenced her with a warning glance. Privately, Natalie agreed with her. There *was* something attractive about Oliver, and he looked as though, with a little assistance from the course, he'd be a very good lover. Not that he held the same fascination for her as Simon did. On the other hand, she was allowed to want involvement with

Oliver, whereas involvement with Simon was forbidden. Unfortunately, the fact that it was forbidden was making it all the more attractive to her.

Rob, who'd been watching proceedings carefully, suddenly stepped forward and tapped Andrew on the shoulder. 'You're trying to make her climax far too quickly,' he explained. 'Melanie, you don't really want his hand between your thighs yet, do you?'

'No,' agreed the brunette.

'If she doesn't hurry up I'll explode,' protested Andrew. 'The way she stripped was enough to drive a man mad. Anyway, she's ready for it. I can tell.'

'Perhaps you didn't hear her right,' suggested Rob, helpfully. 'Melanie said she wasn't ready to be touched there yet.'

'What does she want then?' demanded Andrew.

'Use your imagination.'

Natalie rather doubted that Andrew had very much imagination. Her thoughts were soon confirmed when, after circling her breasts with his fingers a couple of times, he put his right hand down between Melanie's thighs again. 'Get up,' snapped Rob.

Andrew looked over his shoulder at the instructor. 'What?'

'You heard me. Get off her. You didn't do as you were told, which means you have to be punished.'

As Andrew stood in front of Rob, Oliver and Sebastian continued to stimulate their partners. Surprisingly, Oliver's girl seemed a long way from climaxing. But Sebastian's partner's blonde head was beginning to turn restlessly from side to side and she was uttering whimpers of pleasure as he used his tongue to skilful effect on the tips of her nipples. It looked so exquisite that Natalie's own nipples stiffened in response.

Tearing her eyes away from what the other two were doing, she waited to see what Andrew's punishment would be. Rob placed a hand on the back of his neck and pushed his head down, so that he was bending forward from the waist. Melanie then walked behind Andrew, squeezed a little jelly from a tube on to her finger and slowly inserted it between the cheeks of his bottom. Andrew immediately tried to straighten up, uttering a small sound of protest at this unwanted invasion. But Rob's hand remained firmly on his neck.

'What's the matter?' he asked. 'Don't tell me Melanie is doing something that isn't arousing you? Perhaps that's her way of showing you what it feels like.'

'I don't like women doing that to me,' Andrew complained.

Melanie's finger continued to move remorselessly inside the puckered opening and all at once Andrew uttered a cry of alarm. 'God, tell her to stop or I'm going to come,' he gasped.

'You'd better stop, Melanie,' said Rob. 'It seems you did know best, after all.' With a smile Melanie did as she was told, and Andrew was allowed to stand up. His erection was enormous, straining upwards, the veins knotted, and Natalie could see a tiny drop of clear fluid in the slit at the end of the glans.

There's nothing quite like a woman massaging your prostate to make you feel good, is there?' murmured Rob. 'Now, no doubt you're anxious for an orgasm, but I'm afraid you'll have to wait until Melanie's had hers.'

'I'm paying for this weekend,' protested Andrew. 'I don't see why I should—'

'Then leave,' said Rob, calmly. 'The other two guests don't seem to be complaining, but you're under no compulsion to stay'

Like Andrew, Natalie glanced at the other two men. Even Oliver's girl was beginning to move around excitedly, while Sebastian's blonde was obviously on the very edge of a climax. 'You see,' said Rob, 'if you only do as you're told you can soon learn to change your ways and have a much better time.'

'My idea of a good time right now would be to come,' said Andrew.

'It'll be all the better for the wait,' Rob assured him, in a tone that brooked no argument. Reluctantly, Andrew followed Melanie back to the couch and as she lay down on it again he lay on top of her. But this time he used his mouth on her breasts. From the appreciative noises that she quickly started to utter, Natalie assumed that he was making a better job of arousing her this time.

For a few minutes there was silence in the room. But then there was an anguished cry from Oliver's partner. 'You stopped too soon,' she groaned. A muffled exclamation of annoyance came from Oliver.

'What happened, Alice?' asked Rob, pulling Oliver off the blonde girl.

'I was just about to come and he changed the rhythm,' explained Alice.

'My hand was getting tired,' Oliver explained. 'Anyway, I thought she'd like a change.'

'It seems that you were wrong. I'm afraid it's your turn to be punished. A pity: you were doing very well.'

Oliver was less aggressive about this than Andrew had been. Obediently he got off Alice, then stood waiting to see what was going to happen to him. Rob helped Alice up and the pair of them whispered together for a moment. Then, just as Sebastian's partner uttered a cry of ecstasy and spasmed helplessly beneath him as her climax rushed through her, a blindfold was placed round Oliver's eyes and he was pushed firmly to his knees.

Natalie leant forward slightly. The sight of Oliver kneeling submissively at Alice's feet, unable to see, was the biggest turn-on of the morning so far. Heather was equally excited and the two women glanced at each other before looking back at the hapless Oliver. Now Alice pushed Oliver forward until his forehead was touching the carpet, forcing him into a totally submissive position. Rob then handed her a piece of cord with which she tied his hands loosely behind his back, leaving him totally at her mercy. His body was trembling, but whether with excitement or fear Natalie didn't know.

As Rob handed Alice a small riding crop, Heather

drew in her breath sharply. 'I wish they'd let me do that,' she whispered. Natalie didn't answer, afraid that Rob would have them sent out of the room if the sound of their voices shattered its highly charged atmosphere.

As Oliver waited, Alice bent her right arm back and then, with a swift downward motion, flicked the riding crop over his left buttock. He gave a yell of pain, but even before the echoes had died away she'd struck his other buttock. Although he continued to protest, she worked steadily, striking each of his buttocks in turn until his skin began to glow. The blows were clearly hard enough to sting but not sufficiently savage to damage him. It still proved too much for Oliver because soon he started begging for his tormentors to leave him alone.

At a sign from Rob, Alice stopped whipping her victim, dropped the riding crop on the floor and pulled Oliver upright. She unfastened his wrists but left the blindfold on. Now it was possible for Natalie and Heather to see that despite his apparent dislike of what had happened Oliver had actually been very excited by it. The skin of his erect shaft was so tight it looked ready to explode, and his testicles were drawn up tightly beneath the base of the stem.

'Be careful, Oliver,' Rob cautioned him. 'Remember, on no account must you come before you've satisfied Alice.'

'Then let me touch Alice again, please,' Oliver begged. 'I can't wait much longer.'

'I hope you can remember what it was that she liked,' remarked Rob.

Natalie thought that Oliver probably hoped so too, as the blindfold was removed and he and Alice went back to the long couch. As Alice lay down once more, there was a sharp cry of pleasure from Melanie as Andrew finally managed to bring her to orgasm. It had taken him a long time and once or twice, while Oliver had been being punished, Rob had had to go over to Andrew and caution him. But at last he, like Sebastian, had achieved his goal. Now there was only Oliver left.

This time Oliver didn't make any mistake. Natalie quite expected him to begin where he'd left off, with his hand between Alice's thighs. Instead he started by caressing the side of her face and neck, trailing his fingers over her shoulders and the insides of her arms while at the same time he licked delicately at the undersides of her breasts. He also drew each of her nipples in turn into his mouth, sucking on them until her hips began to twitch with pleasure.

Natalie's belly felt tight, and she was hot all over. Watching three women being pleasured, brought to orgasm by men who were being forced to obey instructions, was so arousing that she was desperate for relief herself. Next to her, Heather was surreptitiously caressing her breasts through the thin material of her dress. Clearly she was now even more turned on by Oliver than she had been at the beginning.

Eventually Oliver's hand moved between Alice's thighs again, and as Alice opened her legs Natalie could see that the blonde girl was damp with excitement. Oliver's fingers moved lightly and carefully as he parted his partner's sex lips and began to move his fingers around until he located the place where he'd been before. Immediately she started to twist and turn in a frenzy of excitement. Luckily for Oliver it wasn't too long before Alice gave a scream of delight as the sexual tension of the extended session was finally released in a rush of pleasure – a pleasure that Natalie wished she could share.

'Excellent,' said Rob, the satisfaction evident in his voice. 'Right, now the three of you can make love to your partners any way you wish. But remember that you're being judged and the kind of tutoring you receive over the next day and a half will depend on how you behave now.' Natalie rather doubted that any of the men would listen to anything after they'd heard that they could finally release their pent-up sexual tension by driving their rigid, pulsating erections into their partners.

Sebastian grabbed hold of his girl by the waist and, without any further preliminaries, pushed her against the wall. Obviously used to this kind of reaction, the girl immediately hooked her right leg around his upper left thigh in order to allow him to penetrate her more deeply. One of her arms went round his neck while the other reached round his waist to grip his buttocks so that she could help him move in the rhythm that suited her best.

The frantic urgency of their coupling was very arousing and Natalie began to fidget restlessly as her own need for some kind of sexual stimulation grew. She felt more aroused than she could ever remember and yet she was only watching other people. It shocked her that she could be turned on in this way. She'd never have believed it possible if she hadn't experienced it.

All Andrew did was to get Melanie to lie on her face on the long sofa that they'd been using earlier. Pushing her legs up until she was in a semi-kneeling position, he then drove into her fiercely, almost roughly, making no attempt to caress her in any way. It was clear that his partner's pleasure was no longer of interest to him. He'd forgotten everything in his urgent rush for his long-delayed climax. After little more than a minute he collapsed on to Melanie's back, his breathing heavy and ragged. Watching the pair of them, Natalie knew that there would have been nothing in that for Melanie. Clearly Andrew still had a lot to learn.

Both she and Heather were very interested in Oliver. As soon as the men were given permission to have their own orgasms the other two had rushed towards their goal, but Oliver was different. He sat on the edge of the couch that he and Alice were using and then eased Alice on to his lap, with her back against him. As she rested her head against his shoulder he put his arms around her, his left hand lightly fondling her breasts while his right hand strayed over her hips and down between her thighs.

Natalie's belly tightened and a shiver ran through her as she watched him stroking Alice between her thighs, touching her clitoris lightly so that Natalie's own clitoris swelled and ached as her body craved the satisfaction Alice was being given. Only when Alice had spasmed with pleasure, her whole body trembling, did Oliver start to move her up and down on his erection. It was clear that by this time Alice was as excited as he was because when he finally came she climaxed yet again. With her breasts tingling and an ache between her thighs, Natalie could have wept with frustrated need.

'Interesting,' said Rob, quietly. 'Right, I'd like to talk to you three in private. The rest of you must leave now.'

In a daze of thwarted sensuality Natalie and Heather got to their feet and, accompanied by Simon, walked out into the corridor. Simon looked intently at them. 'I don't really need to ask whether you were affected by that or not,' he remarked. 'Did any one particular man please either of you?'

'I liked Oliver,' said Heather, quickly.

'So did I,' admitted Natalie.

'That doesn't matter,' Simon assured them. 'We'll fix something up for this afternoon. I'm sure that Oliver will be happy to be allowed to take command for a change. After all, we can't have you girls getting too hooked on domination. You're here to learn to be submissive.'

'I'll be submissive for Oliver any time,' Heather whispered to Natalie. Natalie didn't answer, but she was certain that Simon had heard. Having watched Oliver she was inclined to agree with Heather, but she was also nervous at the prospect of her and Heather sharing him whilst Simon looked on.

'We'll meet at two o'clock in my tutor room,' said Simon. 'Until then your time's your own.'

When he'd gone Heather let out a sigh of relief. 'Wow, that was a real turn-on, wasn't it? If Simon hadn't been there I think I'd have asked if I could change places with that Alice girl.'

'You really are keen on Oliver, aren't you?' asked Natalie.

'He's my kind of man.'

'Except that he wouldn't take very kindly to being told what to do.'

'He seems like a quick learner. Alice certainly wasn't complaining. Anyway, by the time I've finished the course here I won't want to keep telling him what to do, will I?'

Natalie wasn't sure. 'That's what they say, but I'm not certain they're going to manage to change me that quickly.'

'At least you've got two weekends in which to learn. I've only got one so I've got to make the most of it,' Heather pointed out.

'I think I'll go and have a shower and change,' said Natalie, who felt an urgent need for some solitude and a chance to think over all that she'd seen that morning.

'Good idea,' agreed Heather. 'See you at two then, in the control freak's tutor room.'

'Do you think Simon's really a control freak?'

'He must be. He takes so much pleasure in his work I can't think of any other explanation. I've decided he wouldn't be my idea of an ideal partner after all.'

'Nor mine,' said Natalie. But in the back of her mind she knew that wasn't really true.

Chapter Seven

Early that afternoon, Natalie joined Heather, Oliver and Simon in the training room. She was the last to arrive and Simon glanced at his watch in irritation. 'You're late.'

'You didn't give me a time.'

'You could have asked me.'

'I thought I was meant to be submissive, following orders. Mind you, it's quite difficult when there aren't any orders to follow,' retorted Natalie pertly.

Simon flushed a little, the cheeks of his normally pale face turning pink. 'At least you're here now. Oliver and I have been talking over what I want him to do. You and Heather don't need any instructions, because all that's required from you is obedience. In other words, you will respond to Oliver's actions and you mustn't attempt to take control at any time. Is that clearly understood?'

Natalie glanced at Heather to see if the other woman would object, but Heather merely shrugged in acquiescence. 'I suppose so,' said Natalie, reluctantly.

'That *is* why you're here,' Simon reminded her. 'I want you all to get undressed now, and then lie on the bed. It's large enough for the three of you.'

Natalie could tell that Oliver was eager to get going. Almost before the words were out of Simon's mouth he'd stripped off his clothes and was lying on the bed, waiting for the other two to join him. Heather was nearly as quick, but Natalie found it difficult.

She kept remembering the way the three girls had stripped so sensually that morning, arousing the men, and she longed to do the same. Because Simon hadn't told her to, she knew that she mustn't, but she felt resentful and frustrated at having any restriction placed on her. She wanted to feel a sense of power as Oliver grew hard watching her. But at the moment a sense of power was just what she wasn't supposed to experience.

'Hurry up,' said Simon.

Finally she was naked and joined the other two on the bed. Oliver swiftly positioned himself between the two women and Natalie was once more frustrated when he turned his back on her and lay facing Heather. Immediately his hands began to move over Heather's body and very quickly Natalie could hear her starting to whimper with pleasure. 'You can move yourself against Oliver's back, Natalie,' said Simon, from the corner of the room. Gratefully she curled herself around his lean hardness and started rubbing her pelvis against his buttocks.

Oliver responded by leaning backwards slightly, increasing the pressure for her, and she felt the first darts of pleasure shoot through her pubic mound. Quickly she wrapped her arms around him and then rubbed her breasts against his upper back, until the tips of her nipples were hard and throbbing. She pressed every possible inch of herself against his skin, squirming and wriggling to gain maximum pleasure. All the time Heather's moans of pleasure were driving her on, making her desperate for proper stimulation.

It was clear that Oliver was thoroughly enjoying himself. He used his lips and tongue on Heather's neck, throat and breasts while his hands caressed her lower body until Heather finally climaxed, and the strength of her orgasm made her grab hold of Oliver. For a brief moment the two women's hands met, and Natalie could feel Heather's shudders travelling through Oliver's body.

After bringing Heather to orgasm Oliver turned to Natalie who now, at last, was allowed to enjoy his love-making. She was so frantic for relief from the tension that had built up within her that she didn't mind when his hand went straight between her thighs. In fact, she was grateful, because her clitoris felt huge and was throbbing painfully. Oliver's erection was trapped between their bodies, and she loved the feel of it, the hardness of the rigid stem and the soft velvet skin of the glans.

When Oliver began to suck hard on her tight little nipples she closed her eyes and gave herself over to the wonderful sensation he was giving her. She could tell that her climax wasn't far away, and for the first time since arriving at The Haven she relaxed, allowing herself to be carried along by what was being done to her. Then, without any warning, Oliver's hips jerked violently and he began to groan with pleasure. His mouth left Natalie's nipple and his fingers, which had been playing so skilfully between her thighs, lost their rhythm.

Struggling upright, Natalie looked across his body and saw that Heather had her hand between Oliver's buttocks, which could only mean one thing. Sated herself, she was now trying to give Oliver pleasure by massaging his prostate. But Natalie knew from bitter experience that if Oliver became distracted by the pleasure Heather was giving him she, Natalie, would lose out.

Infuriated by what was happening she reached down between herself and Oliver, until her fingers found the vital spot below the top of his erection. She placed her thumb against the underside of his cock and her fingers on top, just below the swollen purple head, and squeezed. She knew that he'd lose very quickly his urge to ejaculate, but what she hadn't counted on was his groan of frustration at her interference and Simon's furious reaction.

'What on earth do you think you're doing?' he demanded.

'He was about to come,' Natalie explained.

'So what?'

'It was spoiling things for me. It wasn't fair, it was my turn to have an orgasm and—'

Simon glared at her. 'You had absolutely no right to interfere. Thanks to you I've no idea how controlled Oliver is. I wanted to see whether he could bring you to orgasm while Heather was massaging his prostate, or whether he would get sidetracked. You aren't the only person in this room who's here to learn things, you know. It's the same for Heather and Oliver. You're one of the most self-centred people it's ever been my misfortune to have to teach.'

'I'm sorry, but it's what I always do when men are going to come too quickly.'

'Really? In that case I'm not surprised your relationships are somewhat short-lived. Right, off the bed.'

'What do you mean?'

'I mean that for the moment your fun's over. You can come and stand by me. We'll watch Oliver and Heather. Then, since it's clear to me that you're not yet in the least submissive, we'll have to teach you a lesson.'

Natalie knew that Simon was right. She hadn't thought at all about what she was doing. It had been an instinctive reaction, and she wished that she could turn the clock back. Her body still desperately craved relief from sexual tension yet, once again, she was going to be forced to watch rather than take part.

She expected Heather to give her a sympathetic glance. Instead, when the other woman did catch Natalie's eye, she smiled in obvious satisfaction. Clearly she was delighted with the way things had turned out, which only made Natalie all the more annoyed with herself.

Oliver, who'd been lying on the bed in silence while Simon and Natalie argued, seemed relieved that now he had only Heather as a partner. Without any further delay he pushed her on to her back and then kneeled upwards before lifting her buttocks up slightly and balancing them on the inside of his thighs. As he did this he slid slowly into her and Heather rested her legs against his shoulders, caressing the skin at the tops of his arms with her feet. As she moved around, so he moved within her. Then he told her to keep still and leaned back a little, which meant that his erection was pressing hard against Heather's G-spot. She began uttering tiny guttural cries of pleasure, cries that increased in volume the longer she lay there.

Natalie could imagine the glorious, sweet ache that

must be suffusing Heather's lower body, and she stood trembling at Simon's side as she watched Heather's eyelids droop. Heather's breathing quickened and her hands clutched convulsively at Simon's knees as he remained pressed against her G-spot for several minutes. Finally all her muscles spasmed with the deeply intense pleasure that Natalie knew this kind of orgasm gave.

When Heather's body was still, Oliver withdrew without climaxing himself. He then lowered his head and used his mouth on her. Almost immediately Heather started to writhe on the bed as his tongue licked at her highly sensitive flesh. Natalie watched the other woman's hips rising up off the bed as once more her body rushed headlong into ecstatic spasms of pleasure. Only then did Oliver move away from his partner and glance at Simon for instructions.

'You're doing very well, Heather,' said Simon, approvingly. 'It's time for you to get dressed now. Tonight you'll be mixing with a bigger group of people, because I know that I can trust you to continue being obedient. At least, I hope I'm right in thinking that, because if you fail then I shall take the blame.'

'I won't fail,' promised Heather. It was clear from the

eagerness in her voice that she was anxious to meet some fresh partners.

Simon nodded and gave her a half-smile before turning to Natalie. 'As for *you*, I've no idea when I'll be able to let you loose on other people. Perhaps this lesson will help remind you why you decided to come here. Oliver, I want you to stay by the bed, you'll be needed in a few minutes. Natalie, come and lie down with me.'

Even as he was speaking, Simon was taking off his clothes and Natalie's heart started to beat rapidly in her chest. She was half excited and half afraid. Although she was longing to feel Simon's body against hers, she also knew that the lesson would involve more than just pleasure.

Without even a glance at her face, Simon's hands moved over Natalie's breasts. Then he pushed them upwards before bending his head and running his tongue across from one nipple to the other, occasionally allowing his teeth to graze the sensitive tips. Natalie loved this and her shoulders started to wriggle with pleasure. 'Keep still,' said Simon, 'otherwise the lesson will be more severe than I'd planned.'

It was difficult for Natalie to obey him. But she did

her best, although his lips and tongue lingered on her breasts for a long time, steadily arousing her until the tendrils of pleasure began to snake down through her body. Next, he pushed the heel of his right hand against the soft base of her belly, rotating it until she felt the whole of her pubic area start to swell and become damp. His touch was so clever, so knowing that within a few minutes she could feel herself teetering on the edge of a climax. But then, as her muscles started to gather themselves together for the moment of release, Simon withdrew the heel of his hand.

'Let's see how aroused you are,' he murmured, sliding his fingers between her thighs. She felt him touching her moist, slippery flesh. For a fleeting moment the tip of his finger caressed the side of her clitoris and she drew in her breath sharply at the exquisite pleasure.

'She's certainly aroused,' he told the waiting Oliver before rolling Natalie on to her side and lying down behind her. 'Pass me the tube of lubricating jelly on the side there, Oliver,' he commanded the waiting man. Natalie tensed, and Simon's fingers flicked lightly at her buttocks. 'Relax, it will make this much easier for you.' Unfortunately, his words had the opposite effect on

Natalie: this was something she didn't want and had never allowed before, yet she knew it was pointless to protest. This time she had to be obedient or she might well be thrown off the course, a prospect that filled her with dismay.

Carefully Simon parted the cheeks of her bottom. Then Natalie felt some cold jelly being rubbed around the tight little entrance before his finger moved slowly and carefully inside her, spreading the jelly as it went. Instinctively, her muscles attempted to expel him but he merely stopped moving his finger and waited until her muscles relaxed a little before continuing to lubricate her thoroughly, inside and out. Once he was satisfied he told her to sit up. Then he lay on his back, looking up at her.

'I think you know what's going to happen now, don't you?' he asked, softly.

Natalie shook her head, not wanting to believe that what she was thinking might be true. 'No,' she said softly, 'I don't.'

'I want you to lie back on me and let me inside you, where my finger's just been.'

Natalie had never felt so afraid. 'It'll hurt,' she whimpered.

'Of course it won't. Trust me, I've done this many times before. You'll enjoy it, I promise you.'

Natalie glanced at Heather, and the other woman nodded encouragingly. Oliver, already fully aroused, stood waiting for her to obey. Finally, aware that she had no choice, Natalie lay on her back on top of Simon, but with his erection pressed upwards between his front and her back.

'You'll have to help, Oliver,' said Simon. 'Lift Natalie's hips and then lower her down on to me very slowly. Natalie, you must relax more. Breathe through your mouth, that should help.'

Natalie wasn't sure that anything would help. But when Oliver's strong, long-fingered hands gripped her hips tightly she suddenly felt a rush of excitement as she realised what was happening. Here she was, naked, and with two men fondling her. Not only that, if she could only do as she was told then in a few minutes' time they'd both be inside her, and she'd be filled as she'd never been filled before.

Simon's hands spread her buttocks apart and she felt the soft tip of his erection nudging at the lubricated entrance. Oliver held her lower body steady and then Simon thrust upwards with his hips, pushing the tip of his penis past the initially resisting muscles. Briefly she tensed against him, but then a heavy sensation began deep inside her and she started to embrace this strange intrusion. Carefully Oliver and Simon manoeuvred her until Simon was as deeply inside her as possible. Then Oliver kneeled over her, pushing her knees apart and opening up her vulva to him.

Natalie wanted to ask him to touch or suck on her breasts because they were aching and throbbing, but she knew that she mustn't. She could only have what the two men gave her. Oliver seemed to understand. As he rotated his hips, moving his erection round inside her and pressing against the sensitive nerve endings just inside the opening, he lowered his head and sucked on the soft skin of her areolae.

She could hear herself uttering animal-like cries of delight as the two men started to move, slowly at first and then, as it became clear that she'd relaxed, more quickly. It was only when Oliver's movements became more intense that her body started to protest at the way Simon was filling her second, most private opening. She started to whimper – but then the discomfort changed and she felt searing flashes of red-hot pleasure lancing through her.

Natalie had never felt anything like it before, and almost before she had time to realise what was happening the extraordinary sensations caused by what was being done to her overwhelmed her frantic nerve endings. Without any warning a climax tore through her, a climax so intense that she thought she'd faint with the sheer pleasure of it.

When it was over she felt Oliver start to withdraw. Suddenly she didn't want him to: she wanted him to stay there, wanted to continue to be filled. In an instinctive reaction she tightened her internal muscles around him, trapping him in the soft velvet warmth of her.

'No!' protested Oliver. 'I'm not meant to come yet.' But although Natalie heard the words they didn't really register because already her body was climbing towards another orgasm. As Oliver climaxed so did she, and this time she cried aloud with delirious pleasure.

'What did you do then?' asked Simon, as Oliver climbed off the bed and Simon lifted her off him.

'Nothing,' she murmured, still lost in a haze of sensuality.

'What did she do, Oliver?' asked Simon.

'Tightened herself around me, milked me until I came.'

Simon shook his head in disbelief. 'It seems you never learn, Natalie.'

'I didn't mean to do it,' she explained. 'It was all so good that I didn't want it to end.'

'I think I'd better take you back to your room now,' said Simon quietly. 'I shall have to see if a little private tuition proves more effective. After all, you're more than halfway through your first weekend, and yet you still find it impossible to be obedient for more than five minutes.'

'Does that mean you're going to punish me again?' she asked, her mouth dry.

'I'm afraid you haven't left me any choice,' he said ominously. Both Heather and Oliver gave Natalie a pitying look as Simon handed her clothes to her before leading her away.

Chapter Eight

By the time they got back to her room, Natalie was starting to feel annoyed. Although she knew that she'd made mistakes, it still seemed to her that Simon was taking great pleasure in disciplining her.

'Is there something about me that you don't like?' she demanded as they entered her room.

'Of course not,' he replied, shutting the door. 'I don't want you to waste your money, that's all.'

Natalie wasn't convinced. 'What happens now?'

Simon thought for a moment. 'Get on the bed.'

'Dressed or naked?'

'Just as you are.'

Obediently she lay on her bed, acutely aware that in

the rush to leave the training room she hadn't put her underwear on beneath her ice-cream-pink, button-through dress. 'Tell me, do you have a proper job?' she enquired.

'Of course I do,' he said brusquely, catching hold of her wrists and binding them to the headboard.

Knowing that she mustn't resist what he was doing, Natalie decided to continue the conversation to try and distract herself. 'What is it?'

He gave the silk scarf that he was knotting round her right wrist a sharp tug. 'If you must know, I'm a freelance journalist, permanently at the mercy of people like you.'

'I see,' said Natalie triumphantly. 'That's why you don't like me then, because you blame your failure as a journalist on people like me.'

'Who said I was a failure?'

'Your name isn't familiar.'

'Perhaps you read the wrong kind of magazines,' he suggested as he began to fix restraining loops around her slender ankles.

'Tell me who you write for.'

'Most of the broadsheets have used me at one time or another. Anyway, that's quite enough about me. Let me explain what's going to happen next. I don't have much longer to make sure that you've at least learned the basic lessons of obedience. The only way to stop you interfering, it seems to me, is to tie you up – which is why we've moved on to bondage this quickly. You'll be relieved to hear that I'm going to give you a nice time – but only my way'

Natalie started to feel very excited. Their eyes met and she had an odd sensation in the pit of her stomach, a sudden lurching feeling that was how she always felt when she set eyes on a man that she really wanted. A strange expression crossed Simon's face for a moment, as though he too felt something more than professional interest in her. But almost at once his face became impassive again. 'Time to get started, I think,' he remarked. Then he opened the zip holdall that he'd brought with him from the training room.

Carefully he began to undo the buttons on her dress, his fingers lightly stroking her soft skin as his hands worked downwards, and she felt him opening the dress up, exposing her long, lean, naked body beneath. She wished that she could remove the dress altogether, shrug her arms out of it and throw it away. But because she was bound she had to settle for what Simon was doing.

Once her full length was exposed to him he took a

large sable brush from his holdall and, beginning at her feet, proceeded to use it on every centimetre of her skin, using the most delicate of sweeping motions. The sensation was wonderful: Natalie was so excited that when he started to use the brush on the insides of her knees and the tender skin of her inner thighs she began to shake violently. She arched her hips off the bed as her body instinctively attempted to get the brush to touch her higher up.

'I see you enjoy this,' Simon murmured. 'You know, you have a very responsive body. It's a shame that you don't want to learn how to get maximum pleasure from it.'

'I *do* want to learn,' said Natalie breathlessly. 'That's why I'm here.'

'Then play by the rules.'

'Why have you stopped?' she moaned.

'Because I don't want you getting too excited straight away.'

Natalie wanted to scream at him in fury. But instead she turned her head to one side, determined not to let him see the frustration that she knew must be visible on her face. After a few minutes her body quietened and then Simon started to brush her again. This time he moved the soft bristles over her hip bones and the curve of her waist, which made her stomach tighten. She thought that she'd go out of her mind because by now there was a terrible heavy aching between her legs. It was an aching that only some kind of touch would ease, and she knew that Simon wasn't going to touch her there – at least, not yet.

'It feels good, doesn't it?' he whispered.

'It's bliss,' she moaned. Then she felt the brush start to circle each of her breasts in turn until the soft tissue swelled as they became heavy and engorged. Natalie heard herself muttering incoherently, her arms pulling against the restraints as she struggled to move, trying to bring her nipples into contact with the brush. However, Simon had tied her too tightly and, obviously knowing what she craved, he cruelly made sure that her nipples received no stimulation at all. Instead they were left so tight and aching that eventually Natalie gave a wail of frustration.

'What's the matter?' he asked, with mock concern.

'Nothing.'

Simon nodded approvingly. 'That's a good girl. Perhaps, at last, you really are beginning to learn. Now, I think we could do with a change.'

When Natalie heard a low buzzing sound she felt a surge of relief, realising that he was going to use a vibrator on her. This was exactly what she needed, a firmer touch that would trigger her orgasm. At least, that was what she thought she was going to get. But Simon had other ideas.

He used the slim, pencil-like vibrator with all the skill of a torturer, constantly touching and arousing her, but never in a place that would allow her release. He trailed it along the inner creases of her thighs, he lightly stroked her areolae and he even moved it back and forth across the base of her belly. But he never allowed it anywhere near her nipples or clitoris.

Very soon Natalie was going out of her mind with frustration as her hot, tight, needy body wriggled and twisted in despairing attempts to get the elusive touch that she craved so much.

'You look wonderful,' said Simon when he finally switched off the vibrator. 'I wish you could see yourself.'

'I'm glad I can't,' she groaned. 'When are you going to let me come?'

'Not yet.'

He walked away from her for a few minutes. Natalie

realised that he was waiting for her body to come down from the heights it had reached so that when he next touched her there would be no danger of an instant orgasm. Never before had anyone kept bringing her so close to climaxing only to leave her body stranded, teetering on the brink of release. When Simon finally returned to her with a long peacock feather in his hand she gave a groan of despair.

Lightly, insidiously, he stroked her with the delicate point. He twirled it in her belly button until her hips jerked and her clitoris throbbed. He lazily stroked the inner tops of her thighs, even briefly allowing the feather's tip to glide over her swollen sex lips. But even then she was unable to climax. She had no idea for how long he used the feather. Eventually, just as she felt certain that at the very next touch, no matter where it was, her body would explode into floods of pleasure, he dropped the vivid plume, on to her naked belly and then stood looking down at her.

'Right. I'll be back to see you when I've had my tea break.'

Natalie couldn't believe her ears. 'You can't leave me like this!' she screamed.

'Why not?'

'Because I need to come.'

'The wait will make it all the better for you.'

'No, it won't!' she shouted as he began to walk out of the room. 'Come back! You've no idea what I'm going through. Please touch me again.'

'Where?' he asked with apparent interest.

'Anywhere,' she groaned.

'Sorry, that wasn't quite specific enough. I'd have expected someone like you to know exactly what you wanted,' he said with a smile. Then, before she could say anything more, he'd gone, closing her door softly behind him.

It was only when Simon had left that Natalie realised how helpless she was. He hadn't even loosened her bonds a little, which meant that she was unable to move her arms or legs. With no idea of when he was coming back she felt quite frightened. Then, remembering what he'd said about his work as a journalist, her fear began to change to anger. She sensed that this was his revenge, that he was paying her back for all the rejections that he'd doubtless received from female editors. Her anger saved her from becoming too frightened, but it also worked as an aphrodisiac. Although she was no longer being stimulated her body remained aroused. The sensations lessened a little but her jangling nerve endings still clamoured for satisfaction.

Natalie tried to bend her knees, to rock herself back and forth and put pressure on her pubic mound, but there wasn't enough give in her bonds. Her nipples continued to tingle, and there was an ache at the pit of her stomach that refused to go away. The more she thought about Simon and his work, the more she remembered the things he'd been doing to her before leaving. It was as though she could feel once more the gentle caress of the sable brush, the teasing pressure of the vibrator and the exquisite strokes of the delicious pointed tip of the feather that was now lying redundant on her body. It seemed to mock her, reminding her of the pleasure that it had given her earlier.

She didn't know exactly how long she lay there. She guessed that nearly an hour had passed before the door opened and Simon finally returned. Lifting her head from the pillow, she glared at him. 'You took your time.'

'That's no way to greet me. You should be grateful I bothered to come back at all.'

'You could hardly leave me like this. Even Rob Gill must expect his clients to turn up for dinner.'

'Rob wouldn't dream of interfering in my training methods,' said Simon smugly. 'Mind you, dinner wouldn't be the same without you. Besides, there's an interesting game being played tonight and I don't want you to miss that.'

Crossing the room he looked down at her supine body. Then, bending over her, he blew gently on her nipples, which immediately hardened into tight, pointed peaks. 'Goodness, you're still very aroused,' he murmured to himself.

'What did you expect?'

'I've no idea what to expect from you.'

'Well, I hope you're going to—'

Straightening up, Simon looked at her in astonishment. 'I can't believe it. You're still trying to give me orders, aren't you?'

He looked so angry that Natalie lost her nerve. 'No,' she protested vehemently. 'Of course I'm not.'

'Well, that's what it sounded like to me,' he said softly. With a strange expression on his face, he ripped off his clothes. Then, without any preliminaries at all, he lay on top of her and with one quick thrust of his hips was inside her.

Natalie gave a scream of delight. Simon was so big,

so hard, and at last the terrible aching void was filled as he began to move violently in and out of her. She stared up at him. But his eyes were closed and his mouth shut tight with concentration as, with no regard at all for her pleasure, he concentrated solely on his own climax. She could tell that he was angry, but it was also obvious that he was very aroused – and this excited her. Soon she felt her body gathering itself together as her long-delayed climax approached and even though he wasn't touching her anywhere else she didn't mind. This was what she really needed, this was what she wanted, to feel him deep inside her and, as her hips lifted up off the bed, she tightened herself around him. Immediately the first tiny darts of pre-orgasmic pleasure shot through her.

'Yes! Yes!' she shouted and then, at long last, she felt the hot, flooding pleasure course through her body as her frantic nerve endings were finally assuaged by the blissful pulsations of her climax. As Natalie came and her muscles tightened involuntarily around Simon, she felt him shuddering. Then he gave a groan as he climaxed, emptying himself inside her.

Now, at last, he opened his eyes. But there was no tenderness in his expression. Natalie didn't know why, but she'd expected there to be. Although he'd taken her violently, uncaringly, she'd felt certain that this was because he was angry at having feelings for her. Now, looking into his dark, unfathomable eyes, she wasn't so sure.

'I hope that satisfied you,' Simon said, as he withdrew.

Her flesh twitched as she felt him leave her and she wanted to ask him to lie down with her, to make it more personal. But she knew that not only was that against the rules of obedience, it would also be unprofessional. For the first time she was grateful that she would be coming back the following weekend, because she was determined that somehow she'd get to know the real Simon better.

'Well, did it?' Simon persisted.

'Yes, thank you,' said Natalie, deliberately making her voice submissive.

'Goodness, no complaints at all?'

'None.'

'Then I'll have to untie you.'

Natalie glanced up at him as he began to unfasten her wrists. 'You sound quite disappointed.'

'Nonsense. Surprised, perhaps, but not disappointed.'

'Didn't you feel anything at all?' whispered Natalie.

Simon's body became very still. 'What do you mean?'

'Wasn't it special for you?'

'I was simply doing my job.'

'Were you really?'

'I'm afraid I was. I'm sure it would flatter your ego considerably to think that I find you special, but I'm afraid you're typical of the type of women we get here. More obstinate, possibly, but that's the only difference between you and all our other clients.'

'I see.'

'Don't take it personally,' he said briskly, as he removed the last of her bonds and helped her into a sitting position. 'Even if I was interested in you, which I'd like to emphasise I'm not, it wouldn't be allowed. I'd lose my job here if I ever got involved with a client.'

'And your job here means a lot to you?'

'Yes. I get more satisfaction from this than from anything else I do.'

'How sad,' said Natalie.

Simon was obviously surprised. 'What do you mean, "sad"?'

'Well, you can't be any better than the rest of us at

forming relationships if you get more pleasure from this than from anything else you do.'

'We're not here to discuss my private life, we're here to sort yours out. I'll see you at dinner.'

She could tell that he was eager to be gone, but that didn't matter. At least she'd got through to him, rattled his composure a little, and that was what she needed to do if she was to make any progress. 'What did you mean about this evening?' she asked.

'This evening you're in for a rather different experience. It's a way of training both men and women at the same time. The women are put into pairs and then they make love to each other while some of the men watch. The idea is that women get an opportunity to find out what it's like to pleasure and be pleasured by other women, while it's hoped that the men will learn, just by watching, what it is that women really want.'

'I'm not making love to another woman!' gasped Natalie, horrified by the very thought.

'Why ever not? After all, you seem to think that you know your own body best when it comes to men making love to you. Surely a woman will know without you having to tell her.'

'I can't do it,' protested Natalie, trying to visualise the scene that Simon had conjured up.

'In that case you'll have to leave. The class isn't a voluntary one.'

'But I don't want to leave.' Natalie could hear the fear in her own voice, and despised herself for it, but it stopped Simon in his tracks. He sat down on the bed next to her.

'Listen, Natalie. When you decided to come here you made a very courageous decision. You decided that you weren't happy with your sex life and you wanted to change it. The trouble is that when you change old habits it means trying new ones, otherwise you've nothing to replace your old ways with.'

'But I'm not interested in other women.'

'You don't understand what this is all about. Whether you're attracted to other women or not isn't the point. The point is that during your two weekends here you'll experience pleasure, but pleasure given to you in completely new ways. It isn't as though you're going to be locked up in a room with another woman and left on your own. There'll be plenty of men around. I'd have thought that would appeal to you.'

'Why?'

'Think of the power it gives you. The men will all be frantic with desire for you. Surely that will be a turn-on?'

'I want to try everything,' said Natalie truthfully. 'But I don't know how I'm going to find the courage.'

To her astonishment, Simon put his right hand on the back of her neck and gently ran his fingers through her hair. 'I'll be there with you,' he assured her. 'Just think of it as another of my lessons. If you start to lose your nerve, think of me – that should spur you on. I know you believe that I want you to fail, so my presence should bolster your courage. After all, you don't want me to say that I was right about you.'

'I don't want you to keep punishing me,' said Natalie.

'Really?' He gave a laugh. 'I thought you enjoyed it just now.'

He quickly checked his amusement. But for one fleeting moment he'd given himself away and Natalie knew it, even if Simon didn't. 'Well, I suppose I'll just have to hope for the best,' she said.

'That's the spirit. Perhaps you are going to make it, after all.'

'Perhaps I am,' said Natalie. 'I hope that won't be too big a disappointment for you?'

'No, I shall be very pleased for you.'

'And surprised?'

Simon shook his head. 'No, women like you have long since ceased to surprise me.' With that he left the room.

As Natalie showered and changed for dinner she kept remembering his final words. She didn't like being classed as one of a group, a 'woman like you'. She was determined that by the end of her two weekends Simon would see her as an individual. And, she hoped, one that he desired.

Chapter Nine

When Natalie went down to the dining room that evening, she was shown to a large round table where seven other people were already seated, four men and three young women. Remembering what Simon had told her, she studied the other girls carefully. One of them was a small, bubbly blonde with short curly hair. Another had straight, dark hair and soft brown eyes: Natalie thought that she looked like Winona Ryder. The third girl was an Indian, with a beautiful face and a slim figure, whose hair hung down her back in a thick, dark, glossy curtain.

Natalie pulled out a chair. 'Hi, I'm Natalie.'

'I'm Juliette,' said the blonde. 'This,' pointing at the Winona Ryder lookalike, 'is Victoria and—'

'And I'm Sajel,' said the Indian girl, with a smile.

Natalie waited for the men to introduce themselves, but they didn't. Instead, after nodding politely at her, they continued to chat to each other across the girls, clearly more comfortable with men's talk.

'Rude, aren't they?' said Juliette.

'I think they feel uncomfortable,' said Victoria. Her voice was low and attractive. 'They're probably nervous about tonight.'

'Aren't we all?' said Natalie.

'I'm looking forward to it,' confessed Sajel. 'What do you do for a living?' she continued. 'I'm a lawyer and my husband-to-be, Anil, who's sitting across the table from you, is a hospital consultant. Our parents expect us to marry. But he finds me too assertive and, frankly, he's too controlling for me. We both hope that this course will help us get a better balance in our relationship, because we know that we can't disappoint our parents. Somehow we have to make it work.'

Natalie pulled a face. 'That's horrible. It must be awful to marry someone you're not in love with.'

'Not really. In lots of ways we're lucky. We're from similar backgrounds and our families have been friends for years. Anyway, people who marry for love aren't particularly successful at making the relationship work. At least Anil and I know that we have some things in common.'

'But if you don't suit each other in bed ...'

'We find each other attractive,' said Sajel quietly. 'It's only that Anil wasn't expecting a wife to be quite as opinionated as I am. I think that coming here has done him good, because now he understands that I'm not that unusual.'

Looking at Anil, Natalie could see why Sajel would find him attractive. He had a wonderful face and liquid brown eyes. But there was a firm set to his mouth that suggested a stronger character than an initial glance at his face might suggest.

'Who are the other men?' she asked Juliette.

'I only know their names: Toby, Mark and Adam. I think the three of them have had a bad experience this afternoon because I heard Toby telling Adam that if it wasn't for the fact that he wouldn't get a refund he'd have left here by now.'

Natalie laughed. 'That doesn't sound very promising. They must be finding this as difficult as I am.'

'It is hard,' agreed Sajel. 'Who's your personal tutor?'

'Simon Ellis.'

'Is he the tall man, with dark eyes and a pale face?'

'Yes.'

'He's very attractive. What's he like as a teacher?'

'Very demanding.'

'But exciting?'

Natalie decided to be cautious. 'No. We're not meant to find our tutors interesting, are we?'

'No, we're not *meant* to,' said Juliette. 'But that doesn't mean we don't have feelings. It only means we have to hide them. I fancy my tutor something rotten. His name's Shaun, and he's beginning to think that I didn't need to come on this course because I give in to him so easily!'

At that moment the waiters arrived with the salmon mousse. As they moved around the dining room the loud buzz of conversation dropped to a lower level as people started to concentrate on the excellent food and wine. After the mousse there was rack of lamb with a rose-mary-and-red-wine sauce, and for dessert an exquisite lemon crème brulée. The wine, a light, dry Italian vari-etal, complemented the food and also relaxed Natalie. For the first time she began to feel that she was having a holiday, rather than facing three days of exams.

Everyone in the dining room was left to their own devices for nearly an hour after the meal had finished, before the tutors returned to collect their clients. As Simon approached Natalie, she waited anxiously to see which of the other women at her table she was to be paired with. Much to her relief he signalled for her and Sajel to follow him. Somehow she felt that the Indian girl, who clearly wasn't as embarrassed as the rest of them, would make what they had to do much easier.

Simon was carrying two bags of clothes and handed one to each of the girls. 'You can use my teaching room to change in. When you're ready, leave the clothes that you've got on in there and then go down to the end of the corridor. It's the second room on your left. I'll be waiting for you.'

'How many people will there be?' asked Natalie, anxiously.

'I'm not sure. Quite a few, though. Don't worry, you won't be the only girls there. Juliette and Victoria will be alongside you.'

'But will there be more than the four men we met at dinner?' persisted Natalie.

'I'm afraid you'll have to wait until you've changed

143

and find that out for yourselves,' said Simon, not sounding in the least apologetic.

Sajel had already taken her bag of clothes and was walking off, so Natalie decided not to question Simon further. Clearly the events of the evening were meant to be a surprise for her, although she'd never been a great one for surprises. She always liked to have things planned and presumed that this element of uncertainty was an important part of her obedience training.

'What have you got to wear?' she asked Sajel, as the Indian girl began taking garments out of the bag.

'They're like nothing I've ever worn before,' said Sajel, and now she wasn't smiling. Natalie watched as the other girl put on a stunning, tightly laced white basque along with matching briefs, a suspender belt and long white stockings. A pair of white high-heeled shoes completed the outfit. When she was fully dressed Natalie realised how cleverly the underwear had been chosen to show off Sajel's colouring, and how the basque made the most of her slender figure by pushing her breasts slightly together and up.

'I wonder if my outfit's the same,' mused Natalie. 'I expect it is.' She was wrong. Her outfit was completely different: a pale blue nightdress with thin shoulder straps and criss-cross ribbons down the front, it parted just below her crotch, splitting into two halves that, when she moved, revealed the entire smooth length of her legs. Each side of the split skirt was edged with matching pale blue lace, and there was a matching sheer jacket that she slipped on to cover her shoulders. Much to her relief, she also found a small pair of pale blue briefs, which just covered her pubic mound. There were no stockings for her, but she too had a pair of white high-heeled shoes.

'What's this?' she asked, as her fingers felt something cold at the bottom of the bag. Slowly she drew out a tiny chain.

'It's for your ankle,' explained Sajel.

'See if there's one in your bag,' Natalie urged the Indian girl. 'I expect they're a sign of servitude or something.' Sure enough, Sajel found that she too had a silver ankle chain. Quickly she put hers on, and then the two girls looked at each other.

'Have we really got to walk down the corridor like this?' asked Natalie.

'I don't know what Anil will think,' murmured Sajel. 'He's very possessive, and he hasn't been included in any of my training sessions so far. He won't enjoy other men seeing me like this.'

'He might enjoy seeing you like it himself,' laughed Natalie, trying to cheer Sajel up.

Now it was Sajel's turn to be nervous. 'I don't think I can go in there,' she said, her voice little more than a whisper.

'Of course you can,' said Natalie decisively. 'You're a lawyer, an intelligent, sophisticated woman. You know why you're here, and if this is part of our training, then it's what we've got to do. We mustn't let them see that we're afraid.'

Sajel straightened her spine. 'You're right. Let's go.'

To Natalie's relief the corridor looked empty. But then Simon stepped out of a doorway and she felt her heart sink. He nodded appreciatively before standing back to let them in. 'You both look very lovely. Everyone will be delighted,' he said softly.

Because Sajel was hanging back, Natalie walked into the room first. It was a lovely room, high-ceilinged, its windows large and with comfortable antique chairs placed in a large circle. A thick, pale green carpet covered the floor and in the middle of the circle there were piles of brightly coloured scatter-cushions. The circle was large because there were so many men there, and Natalie heard Sajel's quick intake of breath as the Indian girl saw for herself how many men would be watching them. There were at least a dozen, not counting Rob Gill and his assistants.

As the girls walked across the room two of the men stood up and made a pathway through the chairs so that Natalie and Sajel could enter the space in the middle. Juliette and Victoria were already standing there.

Victoria's outfit was hardly an outfit at all. She had on a pair of skimpy high-legged black lace panties and a black lace bra, but with the cups removed so that her surprisingly heavy breasts were ringed by circles of lace, almost as though she were wearing a harness.

Juliette provided a startling contrast. She was wearing a scarlet wet-look playsuit, cut away so sharply that you could see the flesh up to her hip bones. The plunging halter neckline revealed a tantalising glimpse of her breasts, while below that there was a long zip that travelled down her torso and between her legs. Around her wrists were matching red bands, like imitation handcuffs, although her hands weren't fastened. She looked dramatic and very assertive compared with Victoria, who was obviously embarrassed and whose eyes were downcast.

Once all four girls were in the middle of the circle, Rob Gill, who was watching intently, got to his feet. 'Our four lovely young girls are now going to pleasure each other,' he explained to the circle of men. 'I want you all to watch carefully, and to learn from what you see. Many of you complain that women constantly tell you that you don't understand their bodies. They say you fail to please them because you do what you *think* they'll enjoy, rather than what they truly want. Obviously it makes sense that women should know their own bodies well, which is why they ought to be able to pleasure each other quickly, probably using techniques that you either haven't thought of or don't have the patience to try. Are there any questions?'

Toby, one of the men who'd sat at Natalie's table for dinner, lifted a hand. 'I do. How will you know if we've learned anything from this or not?'

'Because you'll be given a chance later on to show us what you've learned.'

'With these girls?'

'You'll have to wait to find out the answer to that,' said Rob. 'Right, girls, on the table over there you'll find plenty of oils and various gadgets that you may wish to use for your mutual pleasuring. You can begin whenever you like, two of you over here on the right side of the circle and the other two over on the left. The lights will be dimmed a little – but not too much, because I want the men to be able to see exactly what's happening. Try and forget the spectators, if you can. Concentrate entirely on giving and receiving pleasure because that way it will be easier for you all.'

Once he'd finished speaking the lights dipped and out of the corner of her eye Natalie saw that Juliette was already pushing Victoria down on to the cushions, before kneeling at the dark-haired girl's side and starting to move her hands over her body. However, Natalie remained standing awkwardly. She simply didn't know what to do.

She saw Sajel look round the circle. Catching Anil's eye, she was immediately galvanised into action. 'Sit down, Natalie,' she said quietly. 'I'm going to relax you with an Indian head massage.' Sajel then put two of the cushions on top of each other before gesturing to Natalie to sit on them. She stood behind Natalie so that the blonde girl could lean back against Sajel's body.

Almost at once, Natalie felt the fingers of Sajel's right

hand lightly ruffling her hair. She moved her hand over the whole of the scalp, centimetre by centimetre, and her touch was incredibly light, her fingers delicate. It was a very pleasant feeling and slowly Natalie started to relax. Now Sajel used both hands, and with her fingers outstretched allowed them to land softly on Natalie's scalp where she would bring her fingers and thumbs together before springing off, only to land in a different position with her fingers once more outstretched. She did this until she'd covered the top of Natalie's head, and now Natalie could feel her scalp tingling.

Next Sajel changed the rhythm and her movements became slower, more tranquil. She placed one hand flat on the top of Natalie's head with her fingers pointing toward the hairline and slowly drew it backwards along the top of the scalp and down into the nape of the neck. She used both hands, following one hand with the other so quickly that it felt as though waves were rippling through Natalie's hair: she couldn't tell where one stroke began and another finished. She closed her eyes, feeling languorous and almost sleepy. Now she could feel Sajel's fingernails touching her scalp in the same wave-like movement. Allowing her head to fall back, she gave herself over entirely to the gentle caresses of the other girl. She wanted the sensations to go on for ever but as soon as she was completely relaxed Sajel's hands stopped moving.

Now the Indian girl eased the straps of Natalie's nightdress off her shoulders, then unlaced the ribbons and let the garment fall to the floor. Then, placing her hands on Natalie's shoulders, she carefully pushed her back, laying cushions beneath her to form a makeshift bed.

'I'm just going to get some oil,' she whispered to Natalie. When she returned Natalie felt Sajel's delicate hands smoothing oil over her shoulders, stroking down the length of her spine and massaging the small of her back until Natalie started to wriggle with pleasure. When she wriggled against the cushions she inadvertently stimulated her clitoris and gave a soft moan of pleasure as darts of excitement lanced through her lower body.

Sajel's slim hands pulled off Natalie's pale blue bikini pants before rubbing the oil into each of her buttocks in turn, causing Natalie to squirm even more. Now she could feel the insistent, demanding throb of desire between her legs as she writhed beneath the other girl's delicate touch.

She was vaguely aware that Victoria was uttering sharp, guttural cries of pleasure from the other side of the circle but she wasn't really interested. All that mattered was the pleasure that Sajel was giving her, a pleasure that she'd never imagined being able to get from another woman.

'Turn over now,' murmured Sajel. As soon as Natalie was on her back Sajel poured some oil over her breasts and then started to massage it into the highly responsive flesh, moving her hands in circles, first around the circumference of each breast and then drawing the circle closer and closer to the nipple. Natalie moaned with pleasure, thrusting her breasts upwards, waiting for the blissful moment when Sajel's hands reached her nipples. The moment this happened – the Indian girl used the end of her fingers to lightly oil the tight little tips before gently pulling and releasing them – Natalie, without any warning, climaxed in a sharp explosion of pleasure that made all her muscles ripple.

Shaken by the force of her climax she turned her head. Despite the dim lighting she saw Simon leaning forward in his chair, watching her intently. Their eyes met and hastily she turned away again, embarrassed that her body had responded so swiftly to a woman's touch when she'd found it necessary to try and instruct nearly every man who'd attempted to give her similar pleasure during the weekend.

By this time Sajel was breathing rapidly and, abandoning her massage, she stripped off her basque and briefs before lying down on top of Natalie. She rubbed her beautiful dark skin against Natalie's creamy flesh and Natalie shivered when their breasts pressed closely together. As Sajel moved herself around on top of Natalie she made sure that their pubic mounds pressed against each other. Now Natalie was almost driven out of her mind, because she longed for the other girl to touch her more intimately, to caress her between her sex lips where her throbbing clitoris was hungrily waiting for attention.

Sajel seemed instinctively to know what it was that Natalie needed. Without a word she slid down the length of the blonde girl's body, parted her legs and then, holding her sex lips open with one hand, she began to flick her tongue against the damp, needy flesh. Her tongue's touch was light, delicate, but also incredibly knowing. She swirled it upwards and then paused teasingly as she reached Natalie's clitoris.

'Please don't stop!' groaned Natalie, her head moving restlessly on the pillows.

'Don't worry,' murmured Sajel. 'I know just how you're feeling. You're going to come now.' Her words alone were nearly enough to trigger Natalie's orgasm, and when the pointed tip of the Indian girl's tongue flicked against the stem of Natalie's clitoris, Natalie screamed. The pleasure surged through her body in a hot, crashing wave that made the tips of her toes and fingers tingle.

All the time Natalie's body was racked with the intensity of her orgasm, Sajel left her alone. But then, when her body became still, she once more placed her mouth between Natalie's outspread thighs. This time she licked and sucked hungrily at Natalie's sex until the delicious tendrils of pleasure began to writhe once more, building swiftly to a crescendo that peaked in an astonishingly short time in yet another wonderful spasm of release.

Exhausted, Natalie stared at Sajel. 'That was so good,' she whispered.

'Now it's my turn,' said Sajel, with a smile, as she arranged herself on the cushions. Natalie had to force herself out of the haze of pleasure that had enveloped her. Half dazed, she looked down at Sajel, uncertain what she should do.

It was obvious that Sajel was very aroused. Her dark nipples were standing out and her breasts were swollen, while her skin was covered with a thin film of perspiration. When Natalie tentatively stroked between the Indian girl's thighs, Sajel's hips jerked and Natalie could feel beads of moisture on the dark, silken pubic hair.

As she tried to think what to do in order to give Sajel as much pleasure as Sajel had given her, Natalie heard a sharp cry from Victoria, followed by gasps of delight. Turning her head she saw Juliette standing astride the dark-haired girl with a latex whip in her hand. There were tiny red lines across Victoria's breasts and ribs, but it was clear from the sounds she was uttering that the whip had triggered an orgasm, an orgasm that went on for a very long time. After watching Victoria, Natalie realised that she should do something different to Sajel, and she went over to the table to see what she could find.

There was a bewildering array of bottles, scarves, silk gloves, love eggs and vibrators and she had no idea what would give Sajel the greatest satisfaction. Then her gaze lit on a pistol-shaped vibrator. Apart from the vibrator itself, which was unusual because beneath the latex covering there were masses of tiny pearls that rippled under the surface when it was switched on, there was also a six-inch vibrating stimulator for the clitoris. This had a soft, jelly-like tip that rotated, with a choice of two speeds. Natalie tried to imagine what it would feel like inside her, and immediately her pelvic muscles tightened. It would feel delicious, she decided. Picking it up, she returned to where Sajel was lying.

Looking down at the Indian girl, Natalie knew from her own experiences that although Sajel was already excited it would still be better for her if Natalie pleasured her a little more before inserting the vibrator. Quickly she poured some oil into the palms of her hands, then massaged Sajel's belly, the tips of her fingers digging deeply into the taut muscles there. When she lowered one of her hands and pressed against the top of Sajel's pubic mound, Sajel whimpered with pleasure.

The other girl's hips were beginning to move and now Natalie felt that she could insert the strange-looking vibrator that she'd chosen. Gently she eased the latex-covered tip inside the girl's welcoming vagina, pressing steadily while slightly rotating her wrist. Sajel, clearly eager to be satisfied, tightened herself around the instrument of pleasure and within a few seconds it was deep inside her. After checking that the soft, jelly-like probe was positioned exactly over Sajel's clitoris, Natalie clicked on the switch.

Holding the pistol-shaped vibrator steady with one hand, Natalie used her free hand to caress Sajel's breasts, stroking them lightly at first but then more firmly. All the while Sajel's moans of excitement were growing louder and Natalie could see the other girl's body tensing as her orgasm approached.

Across the other side of the circle, Juliette was now being pleasured by Victoria. She'd unzipped the red suit and was kneeling between the blonde's legs, obviously using her tongue to very good effect because Juliette was uttering repeated cries of ecstasy and her body shuddered as one orgasm followed another.

For a few minutes Sajel remained on the edge of release, clearly inhibited by the presence of the watching men. Sensing that she had a problem, Natalie increased the speed of the vibrator. Now, as Sajel's clitoris was enveloped in the soft pulsations of the extension tip and her sensitive internal vaginal walls were caressed by the teasing movements of the tiny moving pearls, the sheer intensity of the sensations overcame her inhibitions and at last her body was swept by a deliciously sweet climax. Unlike all the other girls, Sajel was silent in her moment of ecstasy.

Natalie felt very proud of herself. She hadn't imagined that she'd be capable of giving or receiving such pleasure with another girl: it had been a revelation to her. However, she was acutely aware that a great deal of her excitement had been caused by the watchers in the shadows. Although at times she'd almost forgotten them, they'd always been lurking in the farthest corner of her mind. She'd felt as though she'd been on display, demonstrating how well her body responded to being pleasured and exhibiting her own lovemaking skill and her knowledge of Sajel's responses. In a way, she'd been showing off, and showing off for Simon's benefit.

There was a sudden final scream from Juliette, who was twisting and turning on the cushions as Victoria kept her mouth clamped firmly between her outspread thighs. Then the other two girls were also finished and the four of them stood up, looking towards Rob for guidance.

Getting to his feet, Rob clapped his hands softly three times. 'Well done, girls. That's given all the men here a lot to think about. Now, I'm sure you'd like an opportunity to go and freshen up. When you've done that, please return here for the final part of this evening's tutorial.'

Natalie glanced at Sajel. 'I didn't think we'd have to come back.'

'I wonder what we'll be expected to do?' Sajel queried.

There was no time to find out because Simon was clearing a path for them through the circle of chairs. Pausing only to gather up their clothes and shoes, all four girls walked out of the room. Natalie realised how extraordinary it was that she was able to move about freely whilst naked, but somehow after all that had gone before it didn't seem important. Just the same, she was careful to stand as straight as possible, and felt proud of her firm breasts, tiny waist and long legs. 'I think I'm turning into a bit of an exhibitionist,' she confessed to Sajel as they hurried to their rooms.

'I'm not. To be honest, I'm worried what Anil's going to say after what we did.'

'Well, he must know that you didn't have any choice,' Natalie pointed out. 'After all, he watched. He could have left if it had upset him too much. Besides, you both chose to come on the course in order to learn how to change, to give yourselves a better chance of succeeding if you marry. You don't make the rules here, Rob Gill does.'

'I know that,' said Sajel, pausing with her hand on her bedroom doorknob. 'Of course, if you're being rational and logical about it then it shouldn't have made Anil angry. But he's a very proud man and won't have enjoyed other men watching me.'

'He was enjoying watching Victoria when Juliette was using the latex whip on her,' said Natalie.

Sajel was clearly surprised. 'Was he?'

'Yes.'

'Oh well, I'll just have to hope for the best, won't I? Tap on my door when you've showered and we'll go down together. I wonder what on earth's going to happen next.'

'I don't know,' confessed Natalie. 'But for the first time I'm looking forward to a lesson rather than dreading it.'

Sajel smiled. 'Perhaps that's progress.'

'Perhaps it is.'

Chapter Ten

'You decided to get dressed too,' said Natalie with a laugh, as she and Sajel met in the corridor half an hour later. Both girls were now wearing smart evening clothes.

Sajel nodded. 'I thought it would make a nice change for the men,' she joked.

By the time they got to the room where the men were still waiting, Juliette and Victoria were already there. Unlike Natalie and Sajel, they'd chosen to put their costumes back on. 'I wonder what happens now?' asked Victoria quietly.

'I don't know, but it should be exciting,' said Juliette, with a grin.

Rob Gill got to his feet. He looked around the circle of men, most of whom were sitting tensely in their seats, obviously hoping that they were going to be chosen to join in the final part of the lesson. The first man that Rob picked was a stranger to Natalie. Sturdily built and with a shock of blond hair, he was a little older than the other men on the course but definitely attractive.

'Right, Stephen,' said Rob briskly. 'You can take Victoria to your room. There you can make love to her, using what you've learned from the first part of the lesson in order to give her maximum pleasure. No one else will be present, but you'll be filmed and one of the course tutors will be watching you on a monitor. Naturally, if things get out of hand at any point you'll be removed. Not that I'm expecting any problems of that nature, but I want to make it clear to the girls that we're not putting them at any risk.'

Rob then paired Toby with Sajel, which clearly delighted him. He caught hold of Sajel's hand. 'My idea of heaven,' he said enthusiastically.

Sajel didn't look as though it was *her* idea of heaven, and Natalie wondered how much attention Toby had really been paying to what had gone on. Somehow he didn't strike her as someone who was particularly eager to change their ways. On the other hand, she supposed that the same could be said of her.

Natalie didn't know the third man Rob picked, but as he paired him with Juliette it didn't really matter. She waited tensely to see who she was to get. After long deliberation, Rob decided on Anil, and her stomach lurched. She'd been intrigued by him at dinner that evening. Now that she knew they were going to become lovers she felt quite excited. When he put his hand on her shoulder and their eyes met, she got the feeling that he was as fascinated by her as she was by him.

'That's the evening over for the rest of you,' said Rob. 'Of course, there's nothing to prevent you from trying out the techniques that you've seen on some of the other guests here, if that's what they want. I suggest that you all go to the lounge now, where the other girls are. They've been watching some erotic films that are intended to help them understand male sexuality better. With any luck you'll all have a good night. Remember now, breakfast is at eight tomorrow because we have a long final class to fit in before the weekend finishes.'

'I wonder what the films were like,' Natalie said to Anil as she followed him to his room.

'I don't imagine that they were as interesting to watch as you girls were.'

'Sajel was worried you'd be annoyed,' said Natalie.

'Initially I was. Then I reminded myself that we're both sexually sophisticated people who chose to come on this course of our own free will. It's difficult to cast aside ideas that have been instilled into you from childhood, but if we're to get married then I know that we both have to change. Also, I have to understand Sajel better, and I think that tonight has helped me do that.'

Anil's room was at the far end of the same corridor where Natalie had hers. However, his bedroom was entirely different. It was quite opulent: there was a king-sized bed with thick cushions on top of the duvet, and an ornate headboard. Curtains hung from the top of the wall above the headboard and were caught back in drapes on either side. Next to the bed there was a beautiful white chair with a rounded back and arms and a thickly padded cushion on the seat. There was also a bedside table, a chest of drawers and a wardrobe, and several scented candles, which Anil lit before closing the window curtains.

'Where's the camera?' whispered Natalie.

'Camera?'

'Rob said that we'd be filmed the whole time, remember?'

'I've no idea. Perhaps it's behind the mirror on the wall over there. It doesn't really matter, does it?'

'I suppose not.'

'You can't be feeling shy, not after the display you and Sajel put on for us all.'

'Actually,' confessed Natalie, 'I am. I don't know why, but that was different. There were the four of us, and it was quite easy to forget all you men.'

'You mean you'd rather have forty men watching you than one making love to you?'

Natalie shook her head. 'No, that's not what I mean. I just feel odd, that's all.'

'I can understand that. Try to relax. I tell you what, we'll take a shower together. That should help.'

Natalie wasn't sure why she was feeling so tense. It was partly because Anil's dark eyes seemed to see right into her soul, and she felt a little guilty that she was attracted to him when he and Sajel were probably going to get married. On the other hand, when he stood near to her she could tell that he was already aroused, and so their desire was mutual. If *he* didn't feel that he was betraying Sajel in any way, then it was silly for Natalie to think that she was. 'Shall I undress here?' she asked.

'I'll undress you,' he said. Then, very slowly, his fingers were sliding the short, bolero-style jacket off her shoulders and his hands caressed her bare arms for a few seconds. Next he walked round behind her. Then he nuzzled the nape of her neck as he unzipped her dress. Carefully he eased it down and pressed his hand against her spine so that as she bent forward a little the dress fell off her, slithering to the floor.

She was wearing a cream lacy camisole top and matching panties. Moving in front of her, Anil kneeled down and, with tantalising slowness, drew the panties down over her hips and legs. His tongue followed the path that the panties were taking, so that the soft silken caress of the material moving over her legs was followed by the touch of his tongue trailing a path over the already sensitive skin. He then removed her shoes, her hold-up stockings and, finally, her camisole top.

'There, you're ready,' he said. 'Now I want you to undress me.' She hesitated for a moment. 'Hurry,' he said urgently.

Natalie's mouth felt dry 'I'm sorry,' she apologised, remembering that she must be obedient. She began to unbutton his dark red cotton shirt. But her fingers were shaking so much that she had trouble unfastening it and in the end he had to help her. As she began to remove his belt and unzip his trousers, Natalie's desire for this tall, slim, Indian man increased until she felt herself growing moist between her thighs. He was so obviously in control, but without any of the forceful bluster that so many men used to demonstrate their power.

When she'd finally undressed him, her gaze drank in his lean body, his smooth skin, but above all the amazing length of his cock. It wasn't particularly thick but it was easily the longest that she'd ever seen. Although it wasn't yet fully erect she wondered how on earth she could take him inside her.

'You're beautiful,' murmured Anil. 'Why is it so difficult for you to abdicate control?'

'It isn't any more,' she assured him.

'But it is. I can see the conflict in your eyes, just as I can always see it in Sajel's. Come, let's take that shower now. Perhaps after that it will be easier for you.'

Anil's bathroom was small, but again the overall impression was one of luxury. It had a pale blue thickly piled carpet, a pale blue basin and a large shower cabinet, with plenty of room for two people. Sliding back one of the doors, Anil stood aside and gestured for her to go in first. He then followed her, closing the doors behind him before turning on the spray. Shut in the cubicle with him, Natalie felt afraid. She couldn't believe that they were being filmed here, and she wondered how anyone could protect her if something went wrong.

Fortunately, Anil didn't give her much time to worry. Putting his right hand beneath her chin he tipped her head back a little so that the cascading water trickled down over her face. Instinctively she closed her eyes and felt the water softly caressing her eyelids, mouth and throat.

Anil was standing behind her now, and she rested her head against his chest as he reached round in front of her and started to cover her body in shower gel. The thick, creamy lather smelled of jasmine and once his hands were sliding sensually between her shoulder blades and then down her spine to the curve of her buttocks, Natalie felt her tight muscles start to relax.

Crouching down Anil lathered the backs of her legs, then lifted each of her feet in turn, spreading the creamy suds over the sensitive instep and between her toes before reaching round in front of her. She trembled with excitement as his hands began a slow journey up over the fronts of her legs, her belly, ribcage and finally her breasts. She wished that he'd touched her between her thighs, arousing her with smooth, slippery movements of his fingers, but clearly he intended to make her wait for that pleasure.

His hands were firm on her breasts, but not unpleasantly so. Unlike a lot of men he seemed to understand the way she wanted her breasts to be touched. Whilst the palms of his hands pressed the rounded globes firmly he swirled the tips of his fingers around her nipples, and her breath snagged in her throat with delight.

After a while, when her skin was tingling and she was breathless with desire, he turned her until she was standing against the wall of the shower and he was in front of her, his hands on each side of her body. At last, with infinite slowness, she felt his erection nudging its way between her sex lips. Desperate to have him inside her she thrust her hips forward, but immediately he withdrew.

'Trust in me,' Anil murmured. 'Believe me, your pleasure will come but you have to trust me.'

'I wanted to feel you deeper inside me,' Natalie moaned. But she knew that he was right. She had to follow his pace, because if she didn't then she was falling back into her old ways, repeating the mistakes that she'd made with her lovers in the past.

Once she stopped moving her hips, Anil again began to penetrate her. This time she allowed him to set the rhythm and although he teased her, slipping the head of his erection in and out of her several times before finally thrusting fully forward, she didn't complain because all her nerve endings were jangling. It felt as though a hand was tightening the inside of her body, drawing all the muscles up, and a sweet throbbing ache started to spread through her.

Bending his arms, Anil pressed the length of his body against hers, sliding his skin over the soapiness of hers. He moved himself around, so she could feel him moving inside her.

His mouth was against her ear, and as he thrust in and out of her his tongue flicked lightly around her earlobe. Then he whispered to her, 'I want you to come now. I want to feel you shuddering beneath me, tightening around me. Let yourself go. Allow the pleasure to swamp you.'

Anil's words were so unexpected that, as Natalie was already teetering on the brink of a climax, they triggered her release. Obediently, she spasmed as the exquisite pleasure rushed through her.

To her surprise Anil didn't come. Instead he eased himself out of her and then washed all the suds from their bodies before turning off the shower and opening the doors. He then proceeded to dry her with a thick fluffy towel from the heated towel rail. Although he'd completely taken over, she felt strangely comforted by his actions. He was in control, but he was also protecting her, and she'd never felt more feminine or desirable.

By the time he'd dried every centimetre of her, every tiny nook and cranny, she was already aroused again and desperate for more pleasure. He was still fully erect and his cock looked so beautiful that, without thinking, she reached out to touch it. Immediately Anil's fingers closed round her wrist like a vice, but even when he reproved her his voice was gentle.

'No, not until I say.'

'I forgot,' Natalie whispered. Then Anil picked her up and carried her back into the bedroom.

He laid her on the large bed, placing cushions

beneath her buttocks and, after making sure that her head was comfortably settled on the pillows, he fetched a glass bottle of scented massage oil. 'I'm going to rub this all over you, but I don't want you to come while I'm doing it. I want you to save your next orgasm for when I'm inside you again.'

'I don't know if I'll be able to wait that long,' she confessed.

'I hope you can, otherwise the evening may end sooner than I'd anticipated.'

Natalie looked up at him in surprise. His voice was so quiet, his movements so gentle, and yet it was obvious that he meant what he said. Although he certainly seemed to have learned how to excite her body that evening, she didn't think that he'd managed to overcome his desire to be in control all the time. Not that she was too worried, but she wondered what his tutor would think when they saw the film footage.

While Anil's hands glided over her aching flesh Natalie tried to think about other things, to forget the mounting tension in her body. But when he parted her thighs and stroked her outer sex lips she knew that it was going to be very difficult for her not to come.

'You're enjoying this, aren't you?' he said, and for the first time a slight smile played around his mouth.

'It's exquisite,' she gasped.

'Good.' Now, at last, his fingers were moving towards the centre of her pleasure, the tight little bunch of nerve endings that had been throbbing so frantically all the time he'd been massaging her. When he touched the base of her clitoris with the soft pad of his ring finger her whole body jerked with excitement, and she felt the first treacherous darts of pre-orgasmic ecstasy spreading through her pubic mound. 'Be very careful,' Anil cautioned her.

'Then don't touch me there,' she gasped.

'I *like* touching you there. You feel wonderful, so moist and needy. I'm going to lick you now.'

'Oh, no!' cried Natalie. 'Please don't! I shall come if you do.'

'That would be unfortunate,' Anil retorted. Then she felt his head between her thighs and she tensed in anticipation, waiting for his tongue to touch her. When it did it was with sharp, quick, flicking motions. As his tongue drummed against the pulsating bud she felt herself growing hot and her belly tightened. She was dangerously close to coming now and knew that if he didn't stop soon there was nothing she would be able to do to stop her pleasure from spilling over. Luckily for her, Anil recognised this, because just as she was about to pass the point of no return he lifted his head. He then pushed her legs together and up towards her chest.

Natalie uttered a moan of delight as she felt him sliding inside her. As her feet rested against his chest, he slid his hands under her buttocks so that he could move her up and down in the rhythm of his choice. Carefully, slowly, but with increasing intensity Anil began to thrust in and out of her while Natalie rolled her thighs up and down. His liquid brown eyes were watching her carefully until she gave a tiny scream of delight as his cock struck her G-spot with unerring precision.

'You can come whenever you like now,' he said and she was pleased to hear that at last he was breathless with excitement too.

She'd waited so long for her climax that when he gave her permission to come her body hesitated for a moment, as though unable to give itself the pleasure that had been withheld for so long. Then Anil adjusted her position a little. Because his cock was so long he struck her cervix, and as he rotated his hips this deeply satisfying caress released all the pent-up tension that he'd created.

'Yes!' shouted Natalie and then she came in a series of convulsive shudders that were almost painful. So great was Anil's self-control that he still didn't come: only when her body was still again did he think of his own pleasure.

'Tighten yourself around me,' he commanded her. Greedily she obeyed him, because she wanted to feel him inside her for as long as possible, to try and imprint the memory of his long, clever cock on her mind.

When she clasped herself around him and moved her thighs up and down, Anil's head went back and she watched the sinews of his neck tighten and strain before he too was racked with deep shudders of glorious pleasure.

Slowly, reluctantly, Natalie released her grip on Anil. Carefully he withdrew from her, and then lay down next to her so that their faces were almost touching. 'Did you enjoy that?'

'It was wonderful,' she enthused. 'Sajel's very lucky.'

'I haven't finished yet,' Anil murmured as he caressed the lobes of Natalie's ears and the side of her neck. For a time they continued to lie there, but Anil's hands were never still. He traced the outline of every centimetre of her, his fingers flowing over her curves. As he caressed her, so his own excitement grew until, amazingly quickly, she felt his cock starting to stir again.

'Use your mouth on me,' he commanded her and she obeyed with alacrity. This was an order that she was only too willing to carry out. As her mouth closed over the head of his gradually hardening erection she allowed her tongue to tease the flesh beneath the head of the glans. She enjoyed feeling him harden inside her mouth, enjoyed the sensation of power that she experienced as his hips twitched and his breathing quickened. She was so carried away by it all that she began to lick and suck too enthusiastically.

'That's enough,' he said quickly. 'I don't want to come yet.' Reaching down, he grasped hold of Natalie's shoulders and pulled her back up until their faces were level again. Then he kissed her deeply, his mouth firm against hers.

'Sit in that chair,' Anil whispered as the kiss ended. She stared at him uncomprehendingly, her mind miles away as she tried to picture what he and Sajel must look like together. Realising that she didn't understand him, Anil picked Natalie up without any effort at all and placed her in the chair beside the bed, the chair that she'd noticed when she'd first entered his room.

Once she was seated he pulled her buttocks forward until they were on the front edge of the chair and she had to put her arms behind her for support. Swiftly he kneeled down in front of her. Then, grasping her legs, he put them on his shoulders, which meant that he was exactly on a level with her open, hungry sex.

As he slid into her, her head went back in ecstasy, because now he was resting against her G-spot once more, and the aching pleasure made her moan with delight. He stayed motionless for a long time, until the ache was almost painful and she started to whimper with impatience, longing for the ache to turn into pleasure.

'What's the matter?' Anil asked, and she could see from the expression in his eyes that he was teasing her.

'I ... need to come,' she explained haltingly, afraid that he would regard this request as trying to take control.

Luckily for Natalie, it didn't seem to bother him any more. 'I know you do,' he replied. Then, instead of starting to thrust, he clasped his hands firmly under her buttocks, pulling her towards him while at the same time moving until he was sitting on the edge of the bed.

Taken by surprise, Natalie thought that she was going to fall to the floor, but Anil's hands were strong and his grip sure. By thrusting her elbows back behind her until they were resting on the seat of the chair Natalie was able to support her upper body, while her buttocks rested on the bed with Anil's hands beneath them.

Her legs were under his arms, and she bent her knees until her feet were flat on the bed. While he'd manipulated her into this position Anil had remained inside her. This had the effect of stimulating her even further, so that her jangling nerve endings were screaming for satisfaction.

The chair was just near enough to the bed to enable Anil to move Natalie back and forth on his cock, and this time he moved her rapidly, building to a far quicker rhythm than he had earlier. She felt the pleasure spreading up through her belly, and her clitoris started to throb. Bending over her a little, Anil looped his left arm more firmly underneath her buttocks, freeing his right hand to do just that. The moment his thumb touched the base of her clitoris, Natalie's body grew hot and tight. Then, shamingly fast, she was spiralling upwards into dizzy heights of pleasure as she climaxed once more. As her muscles contracted and released around Anil's cock she expected him to come too, but he didn't. Instead, when her body was finally quiet again, he began to use his fingers on her once more.

'I don't think I can come again,' she confessed.

'Of course you can.'

'I can't,' she protested. But already he was dipping his fingers inside her, spreading her own juices up and over the delicate, highly sensitive tissue. Each time he eased a digit into her she shuddered, because she felt so full with the width of his finger on top of his cock.

Natalie thought that she was going to prove Anil wrong, that her exhausted body would fail to give her another climax. But when the tip of one of his fingers slid lightly over the incredibly sensitive opening to her urethra she gasped as a strange, piercing pleasure lanced through her. Her lower belly felt full and pressurised, as though she could explode at any moment. When he continued to manipulate around the tiny opening a deep, hot feeling spread through her lower body. She could hear herself uttering whimpering sounds, her hips moved restlessly and her body struggled to come to terms with these new sensations.

Her upper body was almost flat on the chair now and she was desperate for the pleasure that her tired flesh seemed unable to give her. Finally, one of Anil's fingers began to stroke the side of the stem of her clitoris, and at last she felt the hot tightness spreading until the blissful pleasure swept through her and her whole body shook violently with yet another climax.

'Now it's my turn,' said Anil, pulling her up against him so that her breasts were rubbing against his chest. 'Keep your legs tightly around my waist,' he added. Then, as she rested her hands on his shoulders, he moved her up and down. He moved slowly at first but with increasing speed, and she stared into his eyes, watching them widen as he finally spilled himself inside her again.

Natalie couldn't remember any other man ever giving her so much pleasure. She wanted to tell him this, but something held her back. She sensed that Anil wouldn't want to hear it, that through simply watching her reactions he knew, and to say anything might endanger his relationship with Sajel.

'I hope we both passed,' he said lightly, in an obvious

attempt to break the intimate atmosphere that they'd created.

'Passed what?' queried Natalie, still not fully concentrating because her body felt so sated that she could hardly make her brain function.

'The camera test.'

Natalie had forgotten all about the watching camera. But suddenly she remembered that Simon had been watching her on the monitor. That he'd seen just how totally she had abandoned herself to Anil. She wondered what he thought of her now.

'I'm sure you passed,' she said, bending forward and kissing Anil in the middle of his forehead.

'I hope so. Unlike you, I don't have another weekend in which to learn.'

'Well, as I said, I envy Sajel.'

'That's nice. However, since you're not Sajel I can't be sure that I've learned enough to make her happy, can I?'

'I think you have.'

'But you relinquished control,' pointed out Anil. 'Sajel finds that very difficult.'

'*I*'ve always found it very difficult before.'

'Then the course is working for you.'

'I suppose so.'

He looked thoughtfully at her. 'Yes, Natalie, it's the course, not me. There's nothing that special about me. In any case, I think your interests lie elsewhere.'

'What do you mean?'

'You don't need me to tell you.'

Natalie felt her cheeks start to redden, because she knew that he was right. As she was already trying to imagine what effect her sex with Anil would have had on Simon, she had to admit to herself that she was clearly obsessed with the man, even if it was forbidden. 'I've no idea what you're talking about,' she lied. Then she left Anil lying on the bed and went to shower before returning to her room.

It had been an exciting experience, and she really did envy Sajel but now she was looking forward to seeing Simon the next day. However, she wasn't certain whether she was looking forward to the final lesson of her first weekend.

Chapter Eleven

At seven o'clock the next morning a maid brought Natalie's breakfast to her room. Drawing back the curtains, she placed on the bedside table a tray with coffee, fruit juice, toast and marmalade on it and then withdrew without a word. Apprehensive about what was to follow, Natalie wasn't very hungry. She only nibbled on the toast, but drank the coffee eagerly.

When she remembered the previous night, and the length of Anil's cock, her flesh began to tingle. She quickly pushed the memory away. Anil had only been a part of the course, nothing more. She suspected that despite the progress she'd made she still had a long way to go before The Haven would consider her stay there a success.

No sooner had she showered and dressed than Simon arrived to collect her.

'Good morning. I must say you behaved very well with Anil last night.'

'Thank you,' said Natalie demurely.

'You certainly seemed to be enjoying yourself.'

She couldn't tell from the tone of his voice whether he was pleased or not, but she suspected from the look in his eyes that he wasn't. 'Is there something wrong with that? I thought you'd be pleased with the way I did.'

'I am pleased.'

'You don't look it.'

'This is how I look when I'm pleased.'

'That's how you look when you're not pleased too.'

'I know. It's quite useful to have an expressionless face.'

'Useful in your work, yes,' Natalie agreed. 'It must be a bit of a handicap in your private life, though.'

'We're not here to talk about my private life,' Simon said abruptly. 'Are you ready for the final lesson of the first part of your course?'

'I suppose so. Should I have worn anything special?'

'No,' said Simon. 'This time you'll only be watching. Take careful note of what you see, because when you come back next weekend you'll be taking part in the Sunday-morning session.'

'You make that sound like a threat.'

'I didn't mean to. Of course, it isn't exactly the kind of thing you're used to doing.'

'I don't think I want to hear any more about it,' said Natalie hastily. 'Shall we go?'

Simon's voice was curt. 'Follow me.' He then set off very rapidly down the corridor, so that Natalie was quite breathless by the time they got to the ground floor.

'Where do we go?' she asked.

'We use the lift from here.'

'To go where?'

'To the basement.'

'What's down there?'

'You'll find out.'

The heavy lift doors slid open. For a moment Natalie paused, suddenly very nervous. 'Come on,' said Simon. 'You were the one who was in a hurry to get down here, remember?'

'Is it dark in the basement?'

'Why, are you afraid of the dark?'

'A bit.'

'Don't worry, there has to be enough light for everyone to see what's happening, otherwise there wouldn't be any point in the exercise. Where's your courage now?'

'What do you mean?'

'From what I've heard you're pretty brave when it comes to business.'

'How do you know that?'

Simon looked annoyed with himself. 'Forget I said that. It was out of line.'

'It certainly was. What's my business life got to do with you?'

'Nothing. Like I said, forget I spoke. I apologise. There, does that make you feel any better?'

It would have done if he'd sounded as though he'd meant it, but Natalie could tell that he didn't. It only reinforced what she'd suspected all along: that his feelings towards her were more personal than he wanted her to know. Luckily his words had the effect of giving her the courage to step into the lift, because she was determined to prove that she was as brave in her private life as she was in her business dealings.

The lift began its descent quickly and Natalie's stomach felt as though it was in her throat. With a gasp of fright she clutched at Simon's arm. 'Don't worry, it's never crashed yet,' he said smoothly.

Natalie quickly withdrew her hand. 'It took me by surprise, that's all.'

'I think that this might as well,' he murmured. She felt his hand in the small of her back as he propelled her out of the lift and into a dimly lit stone-walled corridor. Here, down in the basement, there were no luxurious carpets – and, as far as she could see, no windows. It was cold as well as gloomy and she shivered, wishing that she'd put on a long-sleeved top rather than a sleeveless dress. She could hear strange sounds coming from somewhere, moans and cries, but whether of pleasure or distress she couldn't tell. Instinctively she moved backwards a little and bumped into Simon.

'You only have to watch,' he reminded her.

'But what about next Sunday?' she whispered.

'You're not compelled to come back. Of course, you won't get a refund but apart from that nothing terrible will happen to you. Do you want to go and look at what's happening or not?'

Part of her did, but part of her didn't. She had the strangest feeling that although she was frightened, she was being drawn into a world that was going to fascinate her, a world that she *should* reject but was going to embrace. Simon, standing so tall and dark next to her, seemed like a fallen angel, the man who was going to show her a world of forbidden delights and hitherto unknown pleasures.

'Only you can decide.' Simon's voice was unexpectedly gentle.

'Can't you order me to look?' suggested Natalie.

Simon shook his head. 'It has to be your choice, your decision. It's a big step, Natalie. No one can make your mind up for you. We're not here to force people into doing things against their wishes.'

'But I'm here to learn obedience. If you tell me I have to look, then surely it's part of the course if I obey.'

'Not in this instance. Why are you so frightened?'

'I think I'm afraid of myself,' she confessed.

'In that case, you're missing out on a lot of pleasure. Be bold, Natalie. You'll never get another chance.'

She knew that he was right. 'I want to see everything that's happening,' she said firmly and at that moment she heard a man crying out despairingly.

'Fine.' Simon's voice was once more brisk and matter-of-fact. 'There's no point in going to look at room number one: it sounds as though it will be some time before there's any interesting action in there again. Let's try room number three – you should find that fascinating.'

All the rooms had doors like those of medieval prisons – massive, forbidding slabs of smoke-darkened oak, studded with crude great iron nails and banded with broad strips of pitted, dull metal. When Simon pushed against them it was clear that they were heavy, but as none of them was completely shut the sounds were able to travel from room to room, up and down the corridor. The resulting atmosphere was dangerously erotic.

Although there were no windows in the room they entered there were spotlights in all the corners, focused on a large mattress placed on a high wooden base. A man was lying spreadeagled in the middle of the bed, his wrists and ankles handcuffed to the main structure. Natalie thought he looked vaguely familiar, and realised that he'd been one of the men sitting in the circle who'd watched her the previous night.

Whilst watching her he'd looked quite arrogant, and

although he was handsome she'd been relieved that he hadn't been picked as her partner for the night. Now there was no arrogance left in him. His breathing was hoarse and his muscular, naked body was covered in sweat. There were three naked girls on the bed with him. One of them was sitting near his head, a second kneeling between his legs and the third was running her fingers lightly over his belly.

'What are they doing to him?' Natalie asked Simon.

'Ssh!' murmured the other watchers, who were standing in the shadows.

Simon put his mouth right up to Natalie's ear so that he could tell her without disturbing them. 'Ralph knows that he's only allowed to come inside one of the girls,' he explained. 'They keep bringing him to the edge of a climax, but then none of them will sit on top of him. Because of the way he's restrained there's very little he can do about it. If he comes any other way, then he gets punished – and he's already been punished twice this morning.'

Natalie looked at the helpless man and felt her belly stir with excitement. It was obvious that he was very near to coming again. His erection was straining sharply upwards, almost touching his belly, and she could see how tight his muscles were, while the tendons in his neck and arms were like whipcords.

The girl who was sitting near his head sat astride his face and then started to lower herself on to him. 'Make me come with your tongue,' she ordered him, and Ralph began to frantically lick and suck at her, obviously hoping that if he could please her she might take pity on him.

Natalie's own sex started to throb as she watched the girl's eyes begin to close with pleasure while Ralph's tongue worked busily between her thighs. She could see that he knew what he was doing because the girl was very quickly giving excited cries of pleasure and her breasts swelled. After a few minutes she shook from head to toe as he obediently gave her an orgasm.

Breathing heavily, the girl lifted herself off Ralph. Then, kneeling over him, she kissed him deeply on the mouth, so that she could taste her own juices. This excited Ralph even more and his hips jerked as he arched upwards, searching for relief for his tight, swollen, aching cock. But it quickly became obvious that the girls still hadn't finished with him. As the middle girl continued to caress the skin that was stretched tightly over his hip bones, letting her fingers roam into his dark, curly pubic hair, the girl who was crouched between his thighs leaned forward. She then held her large breasts apart and wrapped them around the end of Ralph's erection.

'No!' he shouted. 'Don't do that!' But the girl only laughed. Then she started to run her hands over the outer sides of her breasts, moving them around, up and down the most sensitive part of his erection until, with a despairing howl of anguish, Ralph climaxed.

Natalie watched, fascinated by Ralph's predicament, as he ejaculated over the girl's breasts. But although his sperm had spilled it was clear that he had derived no pleasure from it – because he'd broken the rule.

'Oh dear!' laughed the girl, who was at the head of the bed. 'Poor Ralph – just when you were doing so well, too. Now you'll have to be punished again.'

'How long is this going to go on?' shouted Ralph.

'It goes on until you finally learn to obey,' said a voice from the furthest corner of the room. Immediately Ralph fell silent. After a few minutes the girl who'd been caressing his belly got off the bed, only to return with a small riding crop in her right hand.

Natalie was now so excited that she forgot to feel sorry for Ralph. All she could think about was her own hungry flesh: the prospect of watching the hapless Ralph being punished excited her still further. The riding crop was used skilfully, each of the girls administering three swift blows before handing it on to the next girl. Soon Ralph's chest, waist and abdomen were covered with thin red lines. But, although he cried out in protest every time the crop fell, Natalie saw that he was starting to grow hard again.

'Surely he's not enjoying it?' she whispered to Simon.

'As I told you before, there can be pleasure in pain,' Simon whispered back.

The punishment continued until each of the girls had had two turns with the crop. Then they began to stroke and caress the tethered man. As their fingers tickled his incredibly sensitive testicles he started to give muted cries of anguish. Once more, his pleasure was building.

This time one of the girls positioned herself above his rigid cock. Very slowly she lowered herself on to him, allowing the tip to enter her, but then quickly raising herself, leaving him straining upwards, desperately trying to bury himself in her moist, welcoming warmth once more.

'Come on,' said Simon to Natalie. 'They'll keep him in suspense for a long time yet. They're very good at their job. There's something else that you need to see now, something that's happening in room number four.'

Natalie knew that she had to go, had to do as Simon said. But she was reluctant to leave the room because the sight of a man so helpless, and yet so needy, was one of the most exciting things she'd ever seen.

'It looks as though you were right,' said Simon, as they walked down the corridor to room number four.

'Right about what?'

'Being afraid of yourself.' With that he opened the heavy wooden door and then stood back to allow Natalie to enter first.

If anything this room was even darker than the first. The spotlights were less bright, and at first Natalie's eyes had difficulty in adjusting. She could tell from the atmosphere in the room that something very exciting was happening, and she could also hear whimpers of sexual arousal coming from a girl somewhere. It was only when her eyes finally adapted to the gloom that she was able to make out what was happening.

A tall, voluptuous brunette was standing on tiptoe, handcuffed to an overhead beam. She was completely naked except for a pair of black, lacy hold-up stockings and stiletto shoes. Standing next to her, one arm around her waist in an apparently tender gesture, was Rob Gill.

Since it was Rob, Natalie knew that it couldn't really be a tender gesture. Clearly it was Rob who was teaching the brunette some kind of lesson in obedience, and from the look of the girl he was doing it very well.

'What's happening here?' Natalie whispered to Simon.

'It's very simple. Joanne can come as many times as she likes – but she has to ask permission before she does. Her main problem is that she can't bear to do that, and sometimes, knowing Rob, she probably doesn't even have the time. Again, when she disobeys this simple order, she's punished.'

'Is she freed if she obeys?'

'Not straight away. She's down here for a couple of hours.'

Natalie's mouth went dry. All at once she realised that, in a week's time, this could be her. She could be standing on tiptoe, her arms stretched tightly upwards, tethered to a beam, while people watched her struggling both with her own sexuality and her obstinacy.

'I don't know if *I* could ask permission,' she admitted.

'Then next week should be very interesting indeed,' said Simon dryly.

It was clear that they'd entered the room during a rest period because now Rob withdrew his arm and knelt down in front of the brunette.

Tenderly his fingers caressed the silken flesh above the lacy stocking tops and the girl trembled violently, the chains of her handcuffs rattling slightly. Very slowly Rob's right hand moved higher as he caressed the inner creases of her groin. Now she was panting with desire. Finally, but still very slowly, he slid two fingers inside her, moving them around and pressing firmly against her inner vaginal walls.

The brunette's whole body began to quake and Natalie could feel her own panties becoming wet as her flesh responded to the caresses she was watching. Keeping two fingers inside the tethered girl, Rob slid his thumb upwards towards her clitoris. Natalie tried to imagine how it must feel to wait, unable to hurry Rob and trying to judge the right moment to ask permission to come.

Whether the brunette refused to ask permission on purpose or not, Natalie couldn't tell, but she suspected not. It seemed to her that the moment the pad of Rob's thumb touched the area around the brunette's clitoris the girl's body spasmed helplessly, not giving her a second in which to ask for permission before her pleasure erupted. For a brief moment she gasped with delight before full realisation of what she'd done sunk in. Then she began to whimper with fear.

'You still forgot to ask,' said Rob quietly.

'I didn't have time,' sobbed the brunette.

Rob stroked the girl's skin, which was covered with a film of perspiration, and brushed her brown curly hair back off her face. He stroked the side of her neck tenderly. 'Then you must learn better control,' he said gently. And as Natalie watched he produced a pair of nipple clamps.

Before putting them on the brunette he licked and sucked at her nipples until they were standing out proudly. He fastened one clamp on to each of her stiffened teats and stood back to admire the effect. The girl squirmed as the plastic teeth touched the tender rigid nipples, and Rob tugged lightly on the silver chain that was suspended from the clamps. 'You should enjoy those: your breasts are so sensitive,' he told her. Then he ran his hands down her quivering body, cupping her buttocks for a moment as he paused to consider what to do next.

The brunette was quaking with excitement, her body trembling as though caught in a breeze as it hung suspended from the beam. Natalie felt ashamed of herself because of how much the scene excited her. A part of her mind told her that she was wrong to be turned on by it, that this was something that she should reject, but despite this attempt at self-control she couldn't help herself. There was something about the whole situation – the image of the brunette trapped, albeit with her own consent, in the handcuffs while Rob Gill pleasured her – that was incredibly arousing. As for the other onlookers, their excitement only added to Natalie's own.

For a few moments Rob stood behind the suspended girl, lifting her up off the ground and taking her weight for a few seconds before letting her feet touch the ground once more. At which point he took hold of her perfect buttocks again, kneading them slowly and deliberately. All the time the brunette's body continued to quiver as the nipple clamps did their work, making her incredibly aware of her soft, sensitive globes.

Finally, Rob released the girl's buttocks and walked

back in front of her, casually taking off his clothes until he too was naked. It was obvious then that he was as excited as the girl. For a fleeting moment Natalie wondered what it must be like to be the brunette, with all eyes on her as she waited to see what Rob was going to do to her next.

Rob put his hands on the undersides of the brunette's breasts, pushing them upwards until she gasped, but whether from pain or ecstasy Natalie couldn't tell. Then he removed the nipple clamp from the girl's left breast. She moaned with relief as the blood coursed through the sensitive tissue once more and Rob fastened his mouth around it. His tongue licked the tip and the brunette began to shiver.

'I want to come,' she whispered.

'Not yet,' said Rob firmly as he removed his mouth from the sensitive area. Natalie was shocked when he abruptly replaced the nipple clamp and the brunette, despite pleading as she was meant to, was once again left with her pleasure frustrated.

Rob then repeated the process with the girl's right breast. Only this time, when her body began to shake with mounting desire, she didn't even bother to ask for permission to come. Clearly, she understood that permission would be denied: her eyes gazed imploringly at Rob but she never uttered a word. Again the nipple clamp was replaced and he moved behind her once more. His steps were purposeful – and Natalie saw that he was now fully erect.

He slid a small wooden block beneath the brunette's feet so that her arms no longer bore her full weight. Then he parted her buttocks and his fingers began to caress between them. Natalie's own buttocks clenched in an instinctive response to the sensations that she imagined the brunette would be feeling.

After a few minutes the girl began to whimper. 'Please don't *do* this,' she gasped. 'I can't take much more.'

'Of *course* you can,' said Rob smoothly. 'You've nearly completed the course: you understand your sexuality now, and so do we. *This* is what you really like, *this* is how you gain the maximum pleasure.'

'No, it isn't,' cried the brunette. But Natalie could tell that the protest was half-hearted. Clearly the girl knew that Rob was telling her the truth. Somehow, during the course of her training, the girl had learned more about herself than she wanted to. And Rob was determined that she should understand this before she left them. In this way, Natalie saw, the brunette would be liberated, her body free to enjoy sex in ways that she would never have allowed herself before coming to The Haven.

For several more minutes the fingers of Rob's left hand continued to move around and between the girl's buttocks. Then, very slowly, his right arm moved around the brunette so that he was able to stimulate her clitoris at the same time. Once his fingers had found the magic spot, the girl's mouth opened in a gasp of ecstatic pleasure.

Now the brunette was shaking so much that Natalie was afraid she might fall off the wooden block. Rob appeared to have no such fears because, without any warning, he thrust himself abruptly into the girl's anus, slamming his hips up against her so that she gave a scream of shock. But the busy fingers of his right hand ensured that any initial discomfort was quickly dissipated by the delicious sensations that were coursing through her lower belly.

With his left arm, Rob held the imprisoned girl steady as he thrust in and out of her taboo entrance. She began to utter keening sounds of pleasure as the forbidden caresses started to arouse her frantic body even more.

As the brunette continued to moan, a young tutor stepped forward from the shadows and silently removed the nipple clamps so that her nipples were finally free. As the blood rushed into them, forcing them into hard little points, the girl gave a scream. Once again it was difficult for Natalie to tell whether the cry was one of pleasure or pain.

Rob was completely lost in his own rhythm now. He moved around inside the girl's secret opening, rubbing the incredibly sensitive walls of her rectum with his invading cock while at the same time his right hand manipulated the soft, moist flesh between her thighs until she became half-delirious with pleasure.

Natalie felt suddenly afraid for the girl, afraid that she'd forget what she had to do. But the brunette had – finally – learned her lesson. 'Please may I come now?' she gasped, as her body tightened and the soft, pink flush of arousal spread over her chest and throat.

Rob pressed his mouth against her ear. 'Yes,' he whispered. And, to Natalie's astonishment, as the brunette climaxed with a loud scream of ecstasy so too did she. Sharp shards of pleasure pierced through Natalie's pubic mound and up through her lower belly, while her breasts swelled and her nipples throbbed. She climaxed without any warning: her body shook violently, just as the brunette's did as she quivered from head to foot. The sound of her handcuffs rattling against the beam only served to emphasise her position of total subservience.

Natalie's climax ended before the brunette's. She watched the other girl's final spasms of release while Simon stood behind her, his hands on her hips. She could feel his erection hard against her buttocks and realised that he knew what had happened to her. She should have been ashamed, but she wasn't: she felt liberated and all her fear had vanished.

'In a week's time that will be you,' Simon whispered. 'What's more, it won't be Rob standing behind you. It will be me.'

Natalie didn't answer him. But his words conjured up a vision of such dark, exciting eroticism that she wondered how she was going to get through the next week.

As the brunette slumped in exhaustion and Rob started to unfasten her bonds, Simon guided Natalie out of the room. 'I think you've seen enough,' he said, his voice expressionless. 'It's time for you to pack now.

We'll see you again next Friday night. You don't have to stay for the talk since you're visiting us again.'

Natalie turned to him, longing to hear something more, something that would show her she was special. 'Is that all you've got to say to me?'

'No,' he said slowly. 'Don't forget that you have to pay for next weekend before you leave or they won't let you back in.'

His words shattered her. She'd been so sure that he, like she, would be personally looking forward to the next Sunday, that regarding it as a commercial transaction seemed like sacrilege. But there was nothing she could do about it.

Whether he meant it or not, he'd obviously decided that this was how he intended to play it. If there really was anything more between them than the normal relationship between tutor and pupil at The Haven then, clearly, it was going to be up to her to prove it on her next visit.

Chapter Twelve

'Nice weekend?' Natalie's secretary asked her as she arrived at her office the following morning.

'Yes, thank you,' she said, after a short pause for reflection.

'Did you do anything special?'

Remembering the basement, Natalie wondered what Grace would say if she told her the truth. The scenes she'd witnessed there had certainly been special, but not in the way that her secretary meant. 'I had a weekend break in the country, that's all.'

'Well, that's different,' said Grace brightly. 'These days you seem to spend most of your weekends working, judging from the amount of typing I get given on a Monday morning. Does this mean you haven't got anything for me at the moment?'

'It does,' confirmed Natalie.

She wished that she could stop thinking about the tethered brunette, and the way her body had quivered and shaken as Rob had forced her pleasure to explode. That image, together with the one of the bound man on the bed, was still etched incredibly clearly on her mind. 'I'll take my post through with me,' she said, making an effort to get herself back into the mood for work. 'Any important calls yet?'

'Only one from Sara, reminding you that at eleven o'clock today you're seeing that freelance journalist she recommended.'

Natalie frowned. 'I don't remember having an appointment to see any freelance journalist today'

'It was arranged on Friday afternoon, just before you left.'

'What's his name?'

'Sam Tudor.'

'Oh.' For one moment Natalie had nurtured the ridiculous hope that it might be Simon who was coming to see her. But then she realised how silly she was being. He was hardly likely to be interested in working for her when he'd made it clear how much he disliked dominating women, either at work or in the bedroom.

For the next hour and a half Natalie made endless phone calls as she started to pull together the articles she wanted for the next issue of the magazine. Then, far too soon, her phone buzzed.

'Yes?'

'Sam Tudor's here to see you,' said Grace.

'Show him in,' said Natalie, wondering why she was seeing the man in the first place. Sara must have told her that he was good, otherwise she certainly wouldn't have bothered. But she had no recollection of their conversation. Presumably her weekend away had wiped it from her mind.

As the door opened she glanced up. For a moment she thought that her heart had stopped when she saw Simon framed in the doorway.

'Mr Tudor?' she asked.

'That's right.'

'Please sit down. That will be all, thank you, Grace. Oh, perhaps you'd be kind enough to bring us some coffee.'

'I'd prefer tea,' said Simon.

'A coffee for me and a tea for Mr Tudor.' Natalie's voice was icy.

'You don't look very pleased to see me,' remarked Simon, glancing around her office.

'I was expecting to see a Sam Tudor. That's not your real name, is it?'

'No, my real name's Simon Ellis.'

'Then why are you calling yourself Sam Tudor?'

'Because I knew when Sara got me this interview that you were coming for two weekends at The Haven. I figured that you might not be too anxious to see me again, and I wanted to have a chance to show you my work.'

'I imagine your work's good. It must be if Sara recommends you. She's very fussy.'

Simon nodded. 'She certainly is.'

'Meaning?'

He shrugged. 'Nothing special.'

'Is your relationship with her personal as well as professional?'

Simon smiled. 'You know perfectly well that's not a question I can answer.'

'You mean she got to know you through The Haven?' Natalie couldn't disguise her astonishment. Of all the women that she knew, Sara Lyons was the biggest control freak she'd

ever met. The thought of her subjugating herself to a man – any man – was incredible.

'I didn't say that,' said Simon.

'You didn't have to. Anyway, what makes you think that you could write for my magazine? I wouldn't have thought you understood the problems facing highflying businesswomen.'

'On the contrary, because of my work at The Haven I understand their problems very well.'

'I hope you're not writing about The Haven!' exclaimed Natalie.

'Of course not. But I indirectly use some of the things I learn there in my articles.'

'Have you brought one with you?' asked Natalie, as Grace brought in their tea and coffee.

'Sure. It's called "Women Divided".'

Natalie waited for Grace to leave before continuing the conversation. 'It feels strange, talking to you like this,' she confessed.

'Not to me. Perhaps it's because it's difficult for you to feel quite as superior as you normally do when you remember how I've seen you. You mustn't let it worry you. My work there and my journalism are completely separate.'

'No, they're not,' retorted Natalie. 'You've already said that you use The Haven to provide you with facts for your articles.'

'Look, I knew this was going to be difficult for both of us,' said Simon. 'If you'd rather I went, then that's fine. None of this was my idea in the first place. Sara fixed the meeting up without telling me. By the time I got to hear of it, it was too late. I couldn't think of a good reason to turn down the chance of working for such a prestigious magazine.'

'I take it you're being sarcastic,' said Natalie.

'Not at all. Your magazine's one of the big success stories of the year. I'd genuinely love to write for it.'

Natalie wished that she was as relaxed about the interview as Simon appeared to be. The trouble was, he was right. She couldn't get the memory of the things that he'd seen her doing, and the control that he had over her, out of her mind. She felt as though she was sitting naked in front of him, and that made it extremely difficult for her to remain in her business mode.

Running her eyes over the article that he'd handed

her she could see why he had said that his work at The Haven had influenced it. It was an extremely well written piece on the personal struggle between political correctness and their true desires that powerful women faced.

'It's very good,' she said at last, raising her eyes and looking directly at Simon.

'But?'

'But what?'

'I can tell that there's a "but". What's the problem?'

'I don't really think it's suitable for my magazine.'

'Now that's interesting,' said Simon thoughtfully. 'I wonder, could you spare me a few minutes to explain why?'

Natalie wanted him to go, but she lacked the courage to say so. He was behaving very well, and his request wasn't an unreasonable one. It was her answer that was unreasonable, and she knew it. 'I'm a bit pushed for time,' she hedged.

Simon's face became shuttered. 'I see,' he said shortly, getting to his feet. 'Okay, thank you for seeing me.'

'Wait,' exclaimed Natalie.

'What is it?'

'I *should* explain why. Sit down for a moment, please. Anyway, you haven't finished the tea that you wanted so badly.'

Simon picked up his cup. 'What's the problem with the article, then?'

'It's too chauvinistic. I don't have a problem with men writing for the magazine. In fact, I've used several. But they have to be more in tune with the way our readers feel.'

'I *am* in tune with the way your readers feel. I see them every weekend at The Haven. Do you really think that if you don't publish this article it becomes untrue?'

Natalie felt very awkward. 'No, I know it's true. What I don't know is how our readers would react to it. I think they'd feel betrayed.'

'Betrayed by who?'

'By the magazine, of course. This isn't what we're about.'

'I thought you were about the problems faced by successful businesswomen. Well, this is one of them. They're not happy because they don't dare express their true desires.'

'I've never had an article about explicit sex in my magazine,' Natalie confessed.

'It isn't about explicit sex. It's about relationships and the kind of relationships that your readers crave.'

'Would you mind leaving it with me?' Natalie suggested. 'I'd like a little more time to think this over.'

'Sure, that's no problem.'

'I'll be seeing you next Friday, I can tell you then.'

'Certainly not,' said Simon abruptly. 'The type of relationship we have at The Haven would be very difficult to sustain if you arrived telling me whether or not you're willing to become my employer, don't you think?'

'I suppose so,' she confessed. Secretly she'd hoped that he'd agree, for the very reason that he'd disagreed. It would have given her a small advantage over him, something to help her through the humiliations that she guessed lay ahead of her.

'If you don't want it, don't bother returning it. Just let me know,' said Simon.

'I'll decide by Wednesday,' promised Natalie.

'Well, thank you very much for seeing me. I'm sorry about the deception, but I was right, wasn't I? You wouldn't have seen me if I'd given my real name.'

'Didn't Sara use your real name?'

'Yes, she must have done. Of course, at the time it

wouldn't have meant anything to you. When I rang to confirm a time I used "Sam Tudor".'

'And you won't have a problem working for me if I do take the article?'

'No problem at all. I'm good at my job and you're good at yours. That's all that matters in this business.'

'Fine,' said Natalie, getting to her feet and holding out her hand. 'Grace will show you out.'

'Yes,' said Simon. Then he smiled. 'Grace doesn't seem like the kind of girl who's ever going to need to come to The Haven. Is she available, or in a relationship?'

'I've no idea,' lied Natalie. In fact, she knew that Grace had recently split with her boyfriend but she had no intention of letting Simon know. The very *thought* of him asking Grace out for a meal was enough to make her feel jealous. If she had her way, the only person from the magazine he'd ever date would be the owner and editor.

Simon's visit unsettled Natalie and she found it extremely difficult to concentrate on her work for the rest of the day. In the end she gave it up as a bad job and left at five o'clock, taking Simon's article with her.

'Are you all right?' asked Grace.

'I'm fine – a little tired, that's all. I'm taking some work home with me.'

'Could I see the article that Sam Tudor left?'

'No, I'm sorry,' said Natalie. 'That's part of the work I'm taking home with me.'

'I'd like to see it tomorrow.'

'Why the interest? Haven't you got enough to be getting on with? I must be slipping if you're short of work.'

'It isn't that,' laughed Grace. 'We're going out for a meal tomorrow night and I thought it would be nice if I knew what his article was like.'

'He asked you out?'

Grace looked taken aback by Natalie's tone. 'Yes. Is there any reason why he shouldn't have done?'

Natalie forced herself to smile. 'Of course not. I didn't think he was your type, that's all.'

'I thought he was drop-dead gorgeous,' confessed Grace.

'He's rather chauvinistic.'

'Really?' Grace's eyes gleamed. 'That'll make a nice change. I must admit, secretly I'm not too keen on the New Age man. I know I should be. At first I like them,

215

sure, but then they bore me. Of course, it's different for you.'

'Why is it different for me?'

'Well, you don't need protecting,' explained Grace. 'I wish I was more like you, but I'm not.'

'Just because he's a chauvinist it doesn't mean he'll protect you,' snapped Natalie. 'It's far more likely that he'll exploit you.'

'We're only going out for a meal,' said Grace quietly. 'I can't think how he can exploit me at a restaurant. At least he seems the sort who'll pay the bill, which makes a nice change.'

'What was John like?' asked Natalie curiously, pleased that she'd managed to remember the name of Grace's previous boyfriend.

'Oh, definitely New Age man.'

Natalie looked thoughtfully at her secretary. 'Do you think our magazine's relevant to your life, Grace?'

'In so far as it's relevant to anyone's.'

Natalie was astonished by the girl's answer. 'What are you trying to say?'

Grace looked uncomfortable. 'I'm not criticising it at all. I think it's a great magazine, and obviously it wouldn't have done so well if loads of other women didn't agree with me. But although everything it tells us is fine in theory, it isn't always the same in practice.'

'But we talk about the problems that women like us face. Surely one of those is chauvinistic men?'

'I suppose it depends on your definition of chauvinistic.'

'Yes, I think you're right,' agreed Natalie. 'I'll see you in the morning.'

All the way home she seethed with anger, unable to believe that Simon could fancy Grace. Not that Grace wasn't attractive – she was – but she was completely unsophisticated and would present him with no challenge at all. In any case, if Simon felt the same about Natalie as she felt about him then she couldn't believe that he'd be asking anyone else out at this stage. All in all, his visit to the office had totally ruined her day, a day that hadn't been particularly great to start with.

By the Wednesday, Natalie knew that she had to publish Simon's article. It was a very good one: clever, incisive and bound to provoke a reaction, which was important. However, he wasn't nearly as pleased as she'd expected when she rang and told him.

'That's great,' he said casually.

'Is that all you've got to say?'

There was silence for a moment. 'What am I meant to say?'

'I don't know. I suppose I thought you'd be more pleased.'

'It isn't the first time I've had an article published in a magazine. Of course, I'm very pleased that you feel it's good enough for *your* magazine. There, is that what you wanted to hear?'

'I didn't want to hear anything in particular,' snapped Natalie, slamming the phone down.

The rest of the week dragged by. Eventually, after what seemed like an eternity, she found herself once more driving through the Sussex lanes to The Haven. This time she was, if anything, even more nervous than on her first visit. Then she'd been ignorant of what lay ahead of her, now she wasn't. She knew that not only was she going to be tested more severely than the first time, she was also going to finish up in the basement, providing a lesson for other clients to watch and learn from.

'You can always turn back,' she said aloud, her fingers gripping the steering wheel tightly. 'No one's forcing you to do this.'

The trouble was, it was no longer just the attraction of learning to develop her own sexuality that was drawing her to the course. It was Simon. She hadn't dared question Grace about her date with him, and Grace hadn't discussed it either. Natalie thought that she'd probably frightened the girl off with her initial reaction to hearing about it, and so she had no idea what had gone on between the two of them. Grace had seemed extremely cheerful for the second half of the week, but then, she was generally a cheerful girl. Natalie didn't know whether she was imagining that there was an extra spring in her secretary's step or not.

Once again the weather was lovely when she arrived, and the course residents were strolling in the grounds. She didn't see anyone from her first weekend there, but presumed that there must be one or two. She knew that nearly half the guests booked in for two sessions.

This time the girl on reception recognised her. 'Good evening, Miss Bowen. Did you have a good drive down?'

'Very nice, thank you. Am I in the same room as last weekend?'

'Oh no, you have a bigger room this time.'

'Is that progress?' asked Natalie, with a smile.

'You may need it,' explained the girl. 'If you wouldn't mind waiting here for a moment your tutor will come and collect you.'

'You mean Simon Ellis?' asked Natalie, suddenly panic-stricken that she might have been given a new tutor for this visit.

'Of course. We like our clients to have the same tutors whenever they return.'

'You mean that if I come back for a refresher course in a year's time I'd get him again?'

'As long as it was for a refresher course. If Rob Gill felt that you hadn't learned anything during your first two stays here then he'd probably assign you a new tutor. After all, there'd be no point in you wasting your money. Not that I can imagine that happening. Simon doesn't have failures.'

'No, I don't suppose he does,' said Natalie quietly.

'How nice to see you again, Miss Bowen,' said Simon, walking through the front door.

'How was your week?'

'Interesting,' she responded.

'Good. I think it's important to have an interesting job.'

'Well, you've certainly got one here.'

'Yes, indeed. Is it room number seventeen?' he asked the receptionist. She nodded. 'Good, that's the one I requested. If you hand me the key I'll take Natalie up now.'

As Natalie followed Simon along the thickly carpeted corridor and up the stairs her heart began to thump against her ribs. Plucking up all her courage, she decided to ask him a question. 'Is there something special about this room?'

'It's a very comfortable one.'

'That's not what I meant.'

'No, I didn't think it was. Here we are – you can see for yourself.'

Pushing open the door, he stood back to let her enter. It was at least twice the size of the room she'd had on her first visit, and if anything even more luxuriously carpeted and curtained. However, it wasn't the carpet and curtains that attracted her attention. To the side of the room, halfway between the bed and the window, there was a wooden bar suspended from the ceiling –rather like the bars in her school gymnasium as she remembered them.

'What's that for?' she asked.

'You'll find out tomorrow. When you've freshened

up you're free to go down and have dinner whenever you like. Your first lesson is at nine o'clock tonight. It won't be in here, it will be in the other guest's room.'

By now, Natalie knew better than to ask what was going to happen at nine o'clock. 'Where shall I meet up with you?'

'In the small non-smoking lounge. You can get a drink there after dinner if you like. Even if you don't want a drink, it's a very comfortable room.'

'Fine, I'll see you then.'

Reaching out, Simon ran his fingers through her silky blonde hair. 'You're very nervous, aren't you?'

'Yes,' she confessed.

'There's no need to be. You'll soon get back into the way of things. Remember, we're all here to help you.'

'Did you help Grace?' she blurted out, and immediately wished that she hadn't because Simon's face darkened with annoyance.

'How many times do I have to remind you that once anyone enters the doors of The Haven they leave their weekday life behind them? I think you should apologise.'

Natalie didn't feel like apologising, particularly as he hadn't answered her question, but common sense told her that it was the only sensible course of action. 'I'm very sorry,' she muttered.

'I'd like it better if you sounded as though you meant it,' said Simon. 'But I accept your apology anyway.'

'Oh God,' groaned Natalie, as the door closed behind him. 'What have I done now?'

Chapter Thirteen

Natalie arrived in the small non-smoking lounge at ten to nine, anxious not to be late. She'd only eaten a light meal as she hadn't felt hungry, due to a mixture of nerves and excitement. She'd been at a table with two other women and three men, all of whom were first-time visitors, and conversation had proved awkward. She'd wished that Sajel was there again, or Juliette and Victoria.

It was difficult talking to people who were there for the first time, because they had no idea of how the weekend would change them, and Natalie knew that she had to be careful not to give anything away. Looking back, she marvelled at how naive she too had been only a week ago, and how much she'd changed. Despite this, she knew that she still had a lot to learn.

'That's nice,' said Simon, as he entered the bar. 'I like women who are punctual.'

'Actually I was early,' she admitted.

'What's the matter, couldn't you wait?' His eyes gleamed with amusement.

'I was anxious to find out what the next lesson would be.'

'Let's get going, then. Tonight I'm going to teach you how to give a man pleasure, but although I'm sure you'll enjoy it I don't expect you to have an orgasm. Is that understood?'

Natalie felt rather annoyed. 'I think I know how to please a man. I didn't come here to find *that* out.'

'You came here to do as you're told,' said Simon firmly. 'Besides, I doubt if you've ever concentrated solely on your partner's pleasure, have you?'

Natalie thought for a moment. 'No, but no man ever expected me to.'

'All the same, he probably wouldn't have objected if you had. I'll be giving you instructions as you go along. Make sure you follow them to the letter. Somehow I don't think that will be such a problem for you in this particular situation, but I thought I ought to remind you that obedience is still the order of the day'

'Is the man a client on the course?'

'No, he's a more than willing voluntary assistant,' laughed Simon. 'Now, that's enough questions. We're using this room.'

The small training room was sparsely furnished, but warm. In the middle of the floor there was a double bed and a man was already lying in the middle of it, completely naked. Natalie thought he was probably about thirty, with light brown curly hair and a compact, well-muscled body. He looked as though he'd done this before, and his eyes seemed to assess Natalie as though he was trying to decide whether or not she would be a good pupil.

'You need to be naked as well,' explained Simon. 'Then, before you begin, I want you to oil your hands, belly, thighs and sex.'

Natalie looked questioningly at him. 'Why?'

Simon sighed. 'Because I say so.'

'I'm sorry,' she apologised. After she'd slipped off her clothes she took the bottle of perfumed oil that he handed her. 'Where do I go to put this on?'

'You don't go anywhere, you do it here. Do it as

slowly and sensually as you can. That should give Craig his first taste of the pleasures that are to come.'

The young man on the bed propped himself up on one elbow. His green eyes stared at Natalie with interest. She felt more embarrassed than she'd expected, not because of Craig but because Simon was standing so close to her. Although he gave no indication that he was in the least bit turned on by the sight of her naked body she knew that he must be. She also knew that the moment her hands started to spread the oil over herself, her body would begin to tingle. Her excitement would be increased by the fact that Simon was watching, but it was an excitement that she would have to suppress since he'd made it clear that during this session it was Craig's pleasure that mattered and not hers.

'Is there something wrong?' asked Simon.

Natalie hastily poured some oil into her right hand and then spread it over her belly. Some of it trickled down the creases of her groin and she shivered as her nerve endings twitched at the arousing sensation. Because of this it was easy for her to move her hand lower, covering her vulva and inner thighs with the sensual slippery liquid. Finally she oiled her breasts and pulled at her nipples, stretching them out as she massaged the oil into them. By the time she'd finished, her nipples were fully erect, the tips tingling deliciously, and she could see Craig's cock starting to stir.

Following Simon's softly murmured instructions she got on to the bed and straddled Craig, who was now lying on his back with his head and shoulders supported on a pile of pillows. Her thighs were over his lower abdomen and she began to massage the oil that she'd previously spread over herself across his chest, shoulders and arms.

Initially Natalie spread the oil with the palms of her hands, letting them slide over his skin. Then, as Craig's eyelids drooped, she kneaded his muscles with her fingers, digging more deeply into his flesh.

After a while, and still following Simon's instructions, she massaged Craig's abdomen in the same way until she could feel his erection pressing up against her. She eased herself back over his thighs a little, sliding smoothly over his flesh because of her oiled body. Then, as his penis stirred and grew, she carefully lowered herself on to the underside of his erection.

She could feel Craig's hips twitching and jerking beneath her as she gently rubbed the underneath of his penis with her vagina. Then, leaning forward, she grasped his wrists and pushed his hands up above his head, holding them firmly against the pillow. Once she had him in this position she was able to move her oiled breasts and nipples over his chest, rubbing herself up and down and from side to side until his nipples too grew erect. The previously flat pink buds had tiny hard points to them, and she shivered as the sweet ache of desire started to grow deep within her belly.

Although Natalie was following Simon's instructions carefully, Craig was clearly under no such restraints. In order to increase his own pleasure he raised his knees, which allowed her to slide her oiled thighs up and down his. She balanced herself on his knees, sliding her hands forwards down his taut thigh muscles, and then let her fingers touch the underside of his scrotum. Immediately his already quickening breathing grew faster and his testicles swelled as his climax grew even closer.

Simon's orders became more precise as he carefully followed the progress of the couple on the bed. Natalie found herself slithering up and down Craig's thighs, pressing her genitals close to his until his mouth opened and he began to gasp with ecstasy. Then she would be ordered to raise herself up once more, and she would have to start massaging his upper torso again until the dangerous point of no return receded. Then she would once more be allowed to rub herself against him.

Natalie was surprised at how turned on she was by Craig's obvious excitement. It wasn't simply the delicious sensations that were caused when she pressed herself against him that aroused her, it was also watching his desire mount and knowing that she was giving him such pleasure. For the first time she understood that there could be as much enjoyment in giving pleasure as in simply receiving it, but despite this she ached for a climax of her own. She hoped against hope that Simon would take pity on her and allow her to release all the incredible tension that had built inside her as she'd aroused Craig.

'I'm going to come soon,' Craig groaned as Natalie, momentarily forgetting herself, rocked her pelvis from side to side so that her clitoris was stimulated and her breasts grew heavy with desire.

'I want him to come between your breasts, Natalie,' said Simon. 'It's up to you to decide how to do it.'

Natalie turned her head to glance at him, hardly able to believe that her own pleasure was to be stopped so abruptly in order to satisfy Craig. But the expression on Simon's face was implacable. Clearly it was going to be as he'd said, and tonight she would have to remain frustrated. Despite her best efforts she couldn't repress a small groan of despair as she climbed off Craig. Then, separating his thighs, she knelt between his outspread legs, bent forward from the waist and trapped his straining erection between her soft, throbbing breasts.

As she rubbed at them, moving them around the shaft of his straining cock, she started to tremble. But Craig was so near to coming that there was no danger of her climax being allowed time to build. All the muscles in his body tightened and he groaned with ecstasy. Then, within seconds, his hips were pumping furiously as his body contorted in spasms of rapture and the hot, white fluid pumped out of him and trickled over her breasts.

As Craig gave a sigh of relief and his body relaxed, Natalie felt a surge of resentment because her own body was still so tight and needy. However, Simon didn't give her time to think about it for very long. 'You can go now, Craig,' he said. 'Put on a towelling robe and take your clothes with you. I haven't quite finished with Natalie.'

'You were very good,' said Craig appreciatively to Natalie as he obeyed. 'If we ever meet outside The Haven, you must remind me who you are. We could have some good times together.'

'That's enough,' said Simon, clearly angered by the man's comments. 'You know the rules, Craig. You're not allowed to make assignations with any of our clients.'

'It's a free world,' said Craig and with one final appreciative glance at the naked Natalie he left.

'Well, how did I do?' she demanded.

'Very well. Did you enjoy it?'

'Yes,' she admitted. 'It felt good watching him get so turned on.'

'And it turned you on, too?'

Natalie nodded. 'I don't think you really needed to ask that, did you?'

'It doesn't turn all women on, only the truly sensual ones. I expect you're feeling pretty frustrated right now,' he added. It seemed to Natalie that his voice was more gentle than usual.

'Yes,' she agreed, with a sudden surge of hope.

'So am I.'

'What do you mean?' she asked.

'I mean that watching you with Craig turned me on as well. The only difference is, I can get you to do something about it.'

Natalie stared at him. 'You wouldn't!'

'Of course I would. What's more, I'm going to. Here, let's see you use your expertise on this.'

As he unzipped himself, Natalie stood trembling in front of him, not with fear but with rage. It had been bad enough having to pleasure Craig without getting any satisfaction herself. But to know that she'd turned Simon on and to have to leave the room the only frustrated person that night was almost unendurable.

However, even though she suspected that Simon had added this part of the lesson on for his own gratification she still didn't dare disobey him. If it wasn't on the official agenda, then in a way it was proof that he was more affected by her than he should be. In any case, she longed to take him in her mouth and suck him dry.

Without him having to say any more she kneeled in front of him. She cupped his already tight testicles in her hands for a few seconds before stroking the underside of his rigid erection with her thumbs. Then she enveloped him with her lips.

She ran her tongue around his glans, allowing her

teeth to graze lightly the tender flesh before dipping the tip of her tongue into the slit at its end.

When Natalie did this Simon's hands gripped her shoulders tightly and his legs started to tremble. He was obviously trying to hold back, to make his pleasure last, but she was too clever for him. She closed the fingers of her right hand around his shaft and moved them rhythmically up and down whilst at the same time sucking on the purple tip. She also let the fingers of her left hand stray beneath his testicles to caress his perineum. This combination proved his undoing.

With gratifying speed Simon gave a shout that was half dismay and half pleasure. Then she was literally sucking him dry, just as she'd wanted. Although her own desperate need for a climax still hadn't been eased she had the satisfaction of knowing that for him the pleasure had come far too quickly.

Reluctantly, Natalie released Simon's wilting erection from her mouth and then stood up, her taut, naked body the silent witness to her own arousal.

Simon nodded to himself, and she realised that he knew she'd deliberately hastened his climax because he hadn't allowed her one. Not that he could complain: he hadn't ordered her to go slowly or make him last. All the same, she sensed that what she'd done would go against her the following day.

'Excellent,' he said politely. 'You've grown very proficient at pleasuring men. Tomorrow we'll see how proficient you've become at being pleasured in different ways from those that you were once used to.'

'What's going to happen?' asked Natalie.

'Tomorrow you'll be completely helpless,' said Simon. 'Not helpless in the way that the girl in the basement was helpless last Sunday, but helpless because you won't be able to do anything to control how your pleasure is allowed to build and spill.'

Natalie began to feel nervous again. 'Will it be in a group?'

'No, it will just be you and one man.'

'Is he someone I know?'

'Oh, yes,' said Simon, and now she could detect a distinct note of satisfaction in his voice. 'You know him very well indeed.'

'Is Anil back for a second weekend?' she asked eagerly.

Simon frowned. 'Anil?'

'Yes, you must remember him. We were picked to go together last Saturday after—'

'Oh, yes, of course, Anil. No, I'm sorry to disappoint you but Anil isn't here this weekend.'

'Then who's the man?'

'Why, me, of course,' said Simon. 'Good night.' With that he walked out of the door, leaving Natalie to get dressed and take her throbbing, frustrated body back to her room.

She knew that she would masturbate to a climax when she showered, otherwise she'd never be able to sleep. But the pleasure wouldn't be the same as it would have been had Craig or Simon given it to her. In any case, Simon, with his parting words, had taken the edge off any pleasure that she might give herself. Because now she was very nervous indeed about her next lesson.

Chapter Fourteen

The next morning Natalie awoke with a start to the sound of her door crashing open. She sat up in bed, her heart racing. 'What's the matter?' she asked anxiously, as Simon moved swiftly to the side of her bed.

'Nothing,' he said brusquely, and before she could say another word he'd covered her eyes with a soft blindfold. Fear flooded through her and she reached up to try and clear her vision.

'Don't touch the blindfold,' he warned her. 'If you remove it, then you must leave. It's part of your lesson.'

'What are you going to do to me?' She despised herself for the slight tremor in her voice.

'No more questions.'

With that, he pulled her out of bed and jerked her nightdress off over her head before tying her wrists loosely in front of her with a piece of soft cord. Immediately she felt both helpless and vulnerable. Although her wrists weren't tied tightly, and she knew that it would be possible to free herself, she also knew that if she did then undoubtedly this too would mean that she had to leave. The cord was a symbol of her submission.

Despite understanding the reason for what was happening to her Natalie was still afraid, and her fear increased as Simon manhandled her out of the bedroom. She could hear voices coming from along the corridor as other residents went to breakfast. When Simon removed his hands from her shoulders and stepped away from her she began to quiver with humiliation.

Natalie realised how she must look to other people, standing there totally exposed. But whilst she felt humiliated she was also becoming aroused by the situation. She could feel her nipples hardening and there was a gentle throbbing between her thighs, a dull ache that told her clearly that she was growing excited.

'Are we allowed to touch her?' she heard a man ask.

'Of course,' said Simon.

Instinctively Natalie took a step backwards but almost immediately found herself trapped against the wall of the long corridor. The strange man's hands reached out and caressed her breasts for a few minutes. Then she felt a tongue lick the hard, aching tips of her nipples for a few tantalising seconds before, with a soft laugh, the man moved on.

'Stay exactly where you are,' Simon commanded her. 'I'll be back in about ten minutes.'

'Ten minutes!' cried Natalie. 'I can't stand out here naked for ten minutes!' But her protest was in vain because there was no reply. Now she was left shivering and alone, waiting for Simon's return.

All around her she heard the sound of doors opening and closing, and at regular intervals people walked past her. Occasionally hands caressed her, sometimes women's hands and sometimes men's, but the touches were only fleeting. They were enough to cause her nerve endings to flicker with desire, skilled and knowing but never sufficient to do more than sustain the level of arousal. Arousal that, if she was honest, had begun when Simon had dragged her from her bed.

After a while it seemed that everyone had gone down to breakfast because the doors ceased to open and close and she was no longer touched by anyone. Now Natalie started to feel angry – angry at Simon because of what he was doing to her and angry at herself for becoming aroused. Then, as more time passed, she started to become anxious.

As various emotions flooded through her body, so her sexual arousal grew. She longed for Simon to return and touch her between her thighs, ease the deep, throbbing ache that was starting to drive her mad. But she didn't dare move. She guessed that she was on camera, and that somewhere Simon was watching her on a TV monitor.

Finally, just when she'd begun to think that she was going to have to remove the blindfold, she felt two hands on each side of her waist and jumped with alarm. 'It's only me,' said Simon calmly. 'Sorry I took so long. I had to take a phone call.'

'I don't believe you,' she hissed.

'I wonder why,' he said mockingly.

'I know you wanted to humiliate me,' she said furiously.

'Why would I want to do that?'

'Because you're annoyed with me about your interview at my office.'

There was silence for a moment. Then Simon tweaked her right nipple, far harder than he'd ever done before. She squealed with a mixture of pain and pleasure. 'That was really naughty,' he said reprovingly. 'I don't mix weekday business with my work here at The Haven, and neither should you.'

'I don't believe you.'

'That's your privilege. Come on, you don't want to stay out here all day, do you? People will be coming back from breakfast soon. I want to get you into my tutor room before they do.'

'You're not taking me up there naked,' she protested.

'I can't think who's going to stop me.' With that Simon caught hold of her bound wrists and began to lead her along the corridor and up the stairs. Natalie found it difficult to follow him. It was horrible not being able to see where she was going, and she didn't seem able to move properly because she was nervous about bumping into things. 'There are no cliff edges here, you know,' said Simon. 'You can't fall off anything.'

'Then take my blindfold off.'

'I'm afraid I can't, not until the lesson's over. Mind how you go. Only two more steps and you're on the next landing.'

At last she heard him opening a door. Then he was leading her into what she assumed must be the tutor room, although she didn't know whether it was the same one he'd used before or not.

Abruptly Simon caught hold of her, pushing her down towards the floor until she half fell on to a pile of cushions. As she moved her bound hands around in an attempt to keep her balance she was acutely aware of the silk fabric that covered each cushion. Natalie realised that, because she could no longer see, her sense of touch was keener than normal.

Simon arranged the cushions so that her upper body was supported and then spread her legs before moving away from her.

'Where are you going?' she asked anxiously, afraid that she would be left alone once more.

'It's all right, I'm still here,' he assured her. A few seconds later she felt his hands on her thighs. Then his head was between her legs and he parted her sex lips before flicking his tongue against the stem of her clitoris.

His tongue was freezing cold and she gave a scream of astonishment. After a few seconds, as the intense coldness began to lessen, he closed his mouth around the opening to her vagina and plunged his tongue deep inside her, until she was squirming frantically with excitement. Then, just as her body began to ascend towards a climax, he stopped and pushed her legs together. Frustrated, Natalie let out a whimper of despair.

'Wait just a moment,' Simon ordered her, and when his hands opened her up again she was ready for the coldness of his tongue. However, this time his tongue was very warm, as though he'd had a mouthful of hot tea or coffee. Yet again her flesh was startled, only this time by the unexpected heat.

She could feel herself trembling all over, her body spiralling upwards towards a dizzying climax. When he thrust his tongue inside her she felt the first tiny spasms of pleasure begin.

'That's far too soon,' Simon murmured to himself. Once again Natalie gave a cry of despair as her thighs were pushed together and she was left aroused, frustrated and restless on the pile of cushions.

Once more Simon left her for a while, about ten minutes as far as she could judge. Then, when her patience was nearly exhausted, he returned. Without a word he turned her on to her belly and his strong hands started to massage the muscles around her trapezius before moving down to her buttocks. Soon she was squirming against the cushions, frantically trying to stimulate her own clitoris as his fingers refused to touch her aching, throbbing bud.

'Keep still,' he ordered her. 'I shan't warn you again.'

'I can't help it, it feels so good,' she moaned.

'Well, be careful not to come until I tell you.'

For a long time Simon continued to massage and caress Natalie's back and buttocks. Then his tongue travelled slowly and tantalisingly upwards from the soles of her feet, up the calves of her legs and the backs of her knees before eventually dipping into the tiny hollow at the base of her spine. She could hear his heavy breathing. Clearly his excitement was growing as quickly as hers. But that was no comfort to her: her body felt so swollen with arousal that her skin seemed too tight, and yet he offered her no relief from the incredible tension.

He'd aroused her so slowly and carefully that her whole body was tingling with desire, and when he left her for a moment she felt certain that soon she was going to be allowed her climax. It was only when he returned and started to part her buttocks that she realised that his idea of pleasuring her might not be the same as hers.

Nervously she tensed. Then she felt him spreading a thick lubricating jelly between her buttocks and down beneath her, so that her inner sex lips and the clitoris itself were quickly covered with the cool lubricating jelly. Simply by spreading it over her he aroused her even more, and she moaned with pleasure as delicious hot tingles shot through her.

'You're so wet you hardly need this,' he murmured as his fingers plunged inside her front entrance for a moment. She quivered from top to toe as he pressed lightly against her G-spot, and for one dreadful moment she thought that she was going to come. Then, with a superhuman effort, she distracted herself from the glorious sensations he was giving her and the moment of danger passed.

'Very good,' he said appreciatively. 'Now, let's see how you like this.'

His hands moved from beneath her up to her buttocks once more, and now she could feel something probing at the entrance to her rectum, something large and pointed. She gave a cry of protest.

Simon briefly massaged her throbbing clitoris until

she relaxed again. 'You really must learn to enjoy this more,' he whispered. 'It will certainly be important on Sunday.' Before she could reply, he twisted his right hand and inserted a vibrator inside her back passage. As soon as it was in her he switched it on. It began to throb and pulsate, stimulating the nerves beneath the paper-thin skin. Very slowly the initial discomfort vanished, but the heavy ache between her thighs got worse and she wanted to sob with frustration. She was so close to a climax, yet because her hands were tied she was helpless to even touch herself between her thighs.

'Tell me what you want,' Simon whispered.

'I want to come,' Natalie groaned.

'Then come.'

'I can't! I need more than that.'

'Tell me what to do and I'll do it. When I do, you can come.'

She didn't want to tell him because it made her feel even more helpless, even more under his domination. But after a few more minutes of relentless stimulation by the vibrator between her buttocks she could hold out no longer.

'I want you to touch my clitoris,' she murmured.

'Speak up,' said Simon.

'Why are you *doing* this to me?' she cried.

'Doing what?'

'Tormenting me so.'

'It's all part of the course. Believe me, it isn't personal. I wouldn't dare do this if it wasn't on the agenda.'

'Please, just let me come,' she screamed.

'You have to tell me what to do,' he reminded her.

'Touch my clitoris,' Natalie shouted at the top of her voice. 'I want you to touch it lightly, to tap your finger against it until I climax.'

Immediately Simon slid his right hand beneath her, whilst his left hand continued to grip the vibrator firmly. At last, after all the teasing torment that she'd endured, Natalie felt his fingers sliding upwards over her frantic flesh until he located the hard little centre of her pleasure. As she drew in her breath sharply he very lightly massaged the shaft of her clitoris – and then, as she'd asked, he tapped on it with the pad of his ring finger.

Immediately shock waves of ecstatic pleasure tore through her tormented body, and instantly her muscles contracted in a huge spasm of ecstasy that had her rolling helplessly around on the cushions. All the time she was climaxing the vibrator continued to stimulate the nerve endings in her back passage. This seemed to prolong her orgasm, because she couldn't ever remember one lasting so long.

Finally her exhausted body was still. Simon withdrew his hand from beneath her and at the same time switched off the vibrator. 'There, that sounded good. Now, let's see how quickly you can come again. I think five minutes is a fair time to set you.'

'What do you mean, "set me"?' Natalie gasped. 'You can't expect me to come to order.'

'Of course I can. You can have a two-minute break and then we'll begin again. Only this time I won't be using any vibrator.'

She didn't know what he meant, what he intended to do. All she knew was that at this very moment she couldn't imagine how it would be possible for her to be aroused again in such a short time.

Still unable to see what was happening, she lay waiting. The two minutes passed incredibly quickly because, within what seemed to her like only a few seconds, she felt Simon's hands on her breasts. For a few moments he caressed them. Although initially she didn't respond, once he began to lick and suck at the sensitive flesh she felt her nipples harden.

'You see?' he murmured, his mouth close to her ear. 'It *will* be easy for you.'

Natalie knew that he was wrong. Just because her nipples were hard it didn't mean she'd be able to climax. But then, as she lay waiting for him to touch her elsewhere, he took her by surprise and, grasping her by the wrists, pulled her off the bed.

For a moment she stumbled and fell against him, feeling the lean hardness of his body. His arms went round her body to steady her, and she felt certain that for this brief moment the embrace was personal, that he cared. Then, as though anxious to correct this impression, Simon proceeded to drag her roughly across the carpet and Natalie dug her toes into the soft pile, afraid of what he was going to do.

'Don't start resisting now,' he cautioned her. 'You've done very well so far.'

'I wish I could see.'

'It's better this way. The sensations are more intense.'

It was true. Her body had never felt more alive, but all the same she didn't like being so helpless, and having her hands bound as well increased her sense of vulnerability. It was easy for Simon to half carry her across the room and then stand her with her back against the wall, whilst pinning her hands high above her head.

His whole body was pressed against hers now, and she could feel how excited he was. Moving carefully, he thrust his pelvis against her, slowly and deliberately arousing the first sparks of desire in her tired body. The fact that it was Simon doing this to her, Simon who was pleasuring her, gave her a sense of triumph because this was what she wanted. Natalie wanted to feel him inside her, possessing her, not simply out of duty but from need.

'You've got three minutes left,' he whispered. She thrust her hips forward against him to try and hasten her climax. 'You're not allowed to move,' muttered Simon. 'You have to wait for me to give you pleasure.'

'But that's not fair, not when I've got to come in three minutes.'

'Stop resisting me, stop thinking that you could do this better. I've never known anyone so obstinate,' he murmured. Then she felt his mouth against the side of her neck. His teeth nipped at the skin beneath her left ear and he began to rub himself roughly against her while making deep moaning sounds in his throat.

By this time Natalie was whimpering too as waves of arousal began to flood through her. She could feel her sex lips opening to receive him, desperate for him to fill the hungry, aching space between her thighs. When he abruptly slammed into her she cried out with delight.

'You like that, do you?' he asked.

'Yes,' she groaned.

Immediately Simon's hips stopped moving, so that although she could still feel him inside her there was no other stimulation. She wanted to wail with frustration because she'd been so close to coming, balanced right on the edge of the hot, delicious pleasure. 'I'm sorry,' she gasped. 'I didn't realise that it was wrong to want to feel you inside me.'

To her relief it seemed that her words were all that Simon needed to hear before continuing, because immediately she'd spoken he started to thrust again.

She could hear his breath coming in rapid gasps. As he drove in and out of her, the friction between their entwined sweat-streaked bodies increased the stimulation for both of them so that within seconds they were totally lost in the intensity of their coupling.

Natalie's shoulders were rubbing against the wall. It was difficult for her to get herself comfortable but she didn't care. Simon was taking her so savagely, clearly driven by pent-up desire, that she knew with absolute certainty that she'd been right about him. He *did* feel something for her, something more than he felt for other girls on the course. Realising this, and knowing that he'd now lost control of his own body, Natalie, aware that she was reaching her time limit, tightened her vaginal muscles around him. Immediately, the pleasure that had been flickering deep within her exploded into an all-consuming spasm that raced through her body.

Simon's climax followed only a few seconds later. They both gasped and shook as their muscles contracted in wave after wave of ecstasy until finally they were both still. Natalie slumped against the wall, wishing that she could see the expression on Simon's face.

For a few moments Simon remained leaning against her until his breathing steadied. Then, almost reluctantly, he withdrew from inside her and released her hands. She felt his fingers untying the cord around her wrists. 'You can take your blindfold off now,' he told her, and she was pleased to hear that his voice wasn't quite steady.

Swiftly she removed the dark velvet band from

around her eyes. But she wasn't quick enough because, as she blinked and tried to adjust her vision, Simon turned away, preventing her from seeing the expression on his face.

'Did I manage it in time?' repeated Natalie.

'Of course you did.' Now he had his voice under control again. 'You're becoming extremely proficient in the art of submissive obedience. Let's hope it stands you in good stead tomorrow.'

Natalie stared at him, all the pleasure of the past few minutes vanishing as she remembered the basement. 'Am I really going to be on display tomorrow?' she asked. Simon stared back at her. For the first time he too looked troubled. 'I'm afraid so,' he said gently.

Chapter Fifteen

Simon explained to Natalie that for the rest of Saturday she'd be accompanying him to his other classes. In a way she was relieved that nothing too demanding was going to be asked of her. But in another way she felt a pang of disappointment that she wouldn't have a chance to be intimate with Simon again.

During the morning she watched him running a class for women on their first visit. Most of them struggled initially against the restraints imposed upon them, and several found it extremely difficult to allow themselves to be tied up and aroused without having any control over the situation. As she watched them all battling to subdue their natural inclinations, Natalie remembered how she'd felt on her first visit. She wanted to tell them that what Rob Gill preached was true, that if they would only submit then they'd gain greater pleasure than they could imagine. But she knew that this was something they had to learn for themselves.

In the afternoon she and several other women were taken out into the grounds. There Simon showed them a man tied to a tree, a narrow band of rope fastened around his waist. All of them were allowed to touch and fondle him, keeping him fully aroused for the whole afternoon. It was obvious that this was a man who was used to taking his pleasure as and when he wanted it, because initially he became furiously angry as he was constantly brought close to a climax only to be left stranded at the last moment. As time passed his anger turned to humiliation: when Natalie lightly fondled his swollen testicles and ran her hands over his thighs and buttocks, he pleaded with her to squeeze his straining cock and let him climax.

'That's the first time I've heard you beg for anything,' remarked Simon as Natalie reluctantly made way for another girl to continue the sweet torment of the tethered man. 'Perhaps you're beginning to learn something at last.'

'I wish I'd never come here,' shouted the man.

'Do you mean you want to leave?' asked Simon.

For a moment everyone was quiet, waiting to see if this was one pupil with whom Simon had failed. But eventually the man shook his head. 'I've paid good money for this – I might as well see it through,' he muttered ungraciously.

Simon smiled. 'I think you're beginning to enjoy yourself.'

Natalie suspected that this was true because – although clearly frantic for sexual release – the man's body was quivering with excitement. When one of the girls rubbed herself against his leg until she climaxed his whole body shook with pleasure, despite the fact that he hadn't yet been allowed to come.

Not until an hour before dinner was the wretched man finally allowed his pleasure. Natalie watched, her mouth dry with excitement, as one of the girls took him into her mouth, moving her lips and tongue knowingly over his taut, swollen penis. With a loud moan of pleasure, he jerked his hips violently. As his whole body went tight he shuddered, spasmed and then was finally still.

Leaving him roped to the tree, the women began to

move back to the house to get changed for dinner. 'I'll be coming to see you in your room when you've eaten,' said Simon, catching hold of Natalie's arm. 'There are some last-minute things I need to teach you before tomorrow.'

At ten o'clock that evening, long after Natalie had decided that Simon had forgotten, she heard a light tap on her door. 'Are you still awake?' he called.

Natalie opened the door. 'Of course. You told me that you'd be coming. I didn't dare go to bed.'

'I'm pleased to hear it. Actually, I should have been here earlier. Rob wants you fresh for tomorrow, but I got held up with a particularly recalcitrant pupil. Luckily she's coming to her senses now, but she was even more difficult than you were last weekend.'

By now Natalie knew better than to rise to the bait. She wanted to protest that she'd never been that diffi-cult but kept silent, determined to show Simon how much she'd changed. He looked thoughtfully at her for a moment. 'I think you're a trifle overdressed.'

Without waiting for him to say anything more, Natalie removed her clothes and stood before him. She was surprised that she no longer felt shy and awkward but instead almost proud.

'You wanted to know what the bar was for,' continued Simon, nodding towards the wooden beam suspended from the ceiling. 'It's a small replica of a similar one that you'll be tied to tomorrow. I'm here to get you used to the position you'll be required to assume.'

'I'm not sure I can go through with tomorrow,' confessed Natalie.

'Why not? You're doing so well.'

'It's the thought of all those people watching me, getting turned on by my humiliation.'

'And by your pleasure,' Simon pointed out.

'I think that's even worse.'

'You can't back out now.' Simon's voice was urgent. 'You've come so far, and done incredibly well. Besides, I'll be there watching you.'

'Is that meant to be a comfort?'

He looked a little uncomfortable. 'Well, I *am* your tutor.'

'Nothing more?'

'Come over here,' he said hastily, obviously anxious to change the subject. 'I want you to bend forward from the waist over the bar and then grasp your ankles with your fingers. Do you think you can do that?'

Natalie wasn't sure. But after Simon had placed some padding over the wooden beam she bent her body forward and found that, as long as her upper torso was well over the bar, she was just able to catch hold of her ankles. 'It's not very comfortable,' she murmured.

'It's not meant to be.' With that he walked behind her and she felt his hands moving over the cheeks of her bottom, down the tightly stretched flesh of the backs of the top of her thighs. Then, very slowly, his fingers strayed lower, tickling her pubic hair until she began to grow damp and felt her sex lips start to swell.

'You see, it's not so bad, is it?'

Natalie's body trembled with excitement. 'Not if this is all there is to it,' she admitted.

'It may be a little more complicated than this,' admitted Simon. 'At least you're comfortable with the position.'

She was, but knew that she wouldn't want to stay like it for too long. 'What will happen if I need to stand up and stretch?' she asked, only half jokingly.

'Somehow I don't imagine that will be an option. Right, now I can tell Rob that you're quite supple enough to be the girl on the beam.'

'You mean that if I hadn't been able to do this some-one else would have had to take my place?'

'Yes, but you'd only have been given something else to do. That might have been worse.'

'It might have been better,' she pointed out.

'True. Now, get some sleep. I shall be back to fetch you at six. Rob likes to get everything set up in the basement in good time.'

'Six! What time do the other residents come to watch me being pleasured?'

'After breakfast.'

'But that's three hours later!'

'I shall be with you all the time, getting you in the mood. Goodnight.'

Simon left the room so quickly that Natalie didn't even have time to get off the bar, and she wondered if he'd done that deliberately in order to put her on edge. If so he'd succeeded, because she passed an uneasy night.

When Simon arrived to collect Natalie at six the next morning she was already awake and dressed. 'Bad night?' he asked solicitously.

'I set my alarm,' she lied.

'How very co-operative of you. I don't suppose you

want anything to eat, but would you like a coffee before we go down?'

'I think just a glass of water.'

Simon fetched her one from the bathroom. Then, in silence, they made their way to the basement. Again, she was struck by the darkness of the area, and as soon as they stepped out of the lift she began to shake with fear.

'Be brave,' Simon whispered. 'It's nearly over now. Once you've completed today you'll leave here a full member of The Haven. That means you'll always be able to mix with like-minded people, because you'll be given a list of other members when you leave.'

'You're the only person here that I'm interested in,' said Natalie.

Simon ignored her remark and propelled her hastily towards the room where she was to be on display. 'You can get changed in here,' he said, as they entered the low-ceilinged, dark, stone-walled room. 'You're to put on the suspender belt, stockings and high-heeled shoes. Your clothes will be taken away until you've finished.'

Once she'd changed, Simon made Natalie walk around the room so that he could study her. This time she felt very self-conscious as she paraded in front of him. 'Stand up straight,' he commanded her. 'You should have learned to be proud of your body.'

'Surely you can understand how nervous I am today,' she retorted.

Simon sighed. 'I did think that by now you'd have stopped answering back. Right, this is the beam that you'll be bent over. It's pretty much the same as the one in your room.'

'It's much broader,' remarked Natalie.

'That's to make it more comfortable for you, because you'll be on this one longer. Look, you rest your stomach on the padded part, so that you don't get too uncomfortable. That's right, reach forward and grasp your ankles as you did last night.'

Natalie was so busy worrying about what she was going to look like to the spectators that it was only when she heard the click of the cuffs that she realised Simon had fastened her wrists and ankles together. Now she couldn't move from the position he'd put her in, bending over the bar, her whole body taut and her legs straight.

Moving in front of her, Simon crouched down and began to fondle her breasts with his left hand. He squeezed the soft mounds of flesh until she was moaning with pleasure and then drew each of her nipples in turn into his mouth, sucking on them firmly before tonguing the tight peaks. Delicious waves of pleasure washed through her, and her nerve endings sent piercing shards of excitement through her whole body, right to her very core.

Now Simon moved his right hand up over her stockinged thighs to tug gently on her pubic hair before cupping her vulva, pressing upwards so that the pressure began to build low in her belly.

'You're going to come in a moment, aren't you?' he whispered. 'It's all right, you can because this is just practice. You're not allowed to come once people are here watching, though – no matter what I do to you.' 'But I'm bound to come!' Natalie cried in dismay. 'Of course you are, that's the whole point. Every time you come you have to apologise to me, and ask me to punish you.'

'Ask you to punish me?' she cried, her voice incredulous.

'That's right.'

'That's the most humiliating thing I've ever heard!'

'I know. That's why it's your final test.'

All the time they were talking he continued to massage her breasts with his left hand while his right pressed steadily against her vulva, until all the delicious sensations joined together and a wonderful climax rippled through her. 'I'm going to have my breakfast now,' said Simon, drawing a finger along her spine. 'When I come back I shall be bringing some spectators with me. And then the test really begins.'

When he'd gone Natalie struggled to get more comfortable and then, as her body quietened, she thought back to what her life had been like before she'd come to The Haven. She wondered how on earth she'd ever ended up like this – naked, bound and totally lost in a dark, depraved world of erotic sensuality that she'd never, in her wildest dreams, imagined could have existed.

It was because of Jan that she was here, and now she understood why it was that Jan had changed so much after her own visit. It was impossible for Natalie to imagine returning to her old way of life once her final lesson was over because now her body was used to being pleasured in different ways. It needed the kind of stimulation that she'd been taught to enjoy here. She no longer wanted to control men, because she knew that

MARINA ANDERSON

by subjugating herself to them she got more satisfaction.

Also, it was obvious from the expression on Simon's
face that by subjugating herself she'd managed to
enslave him. She knew with absolute certainty that he
wanted her, and that when he took her the pleasure was
as great for him as it was for her.

She was still trying to work out how her new-found
eagerness to be submissive in her sexual life would be
compatible with her business life when the heavy
wooden door creaked open and Simon returned followed by a group of clients and Marc, who'd watched
her during her very first lesson. Immediately the lighting was dimmed. Then a spotlight was switched on,
shining down on her tethered body stretched tightly
over the wooden beam.

Luckily, because her head was down, she didn't have
to look at the spectators. Instead, she listened as Simon
explained to them that she was not meant to reach
orgasm and would have to beg to be punished if she did
come by mistake or through lack of self-control. Once
he'd finished speaking she heard the low buzz of
excited conversation amongst the onlookers. Then, as
Simon approached her, it all fell silent.

Standing behind her, Simon reached over until his hands rested on her shoulders. Then, very tenderly, he stroked her tightly tethered body. He moved his hands in a steady rhythm, gliding his fingers over her flesh, and occasionally he moved round to the front of her so that he could fondle her breasts.

At first, probably because she was being watched, Natalie was in no danger of climaxing. But as the minutes passed and Simon's clever, knowing fingers kneaded her sensitive breasts and stroked her lower belly beneath the bar, so the first tingles of excitement coursed through her.

Once again Simon used his mouth on her breasts. This time when her nipples swelled he nibbled on them with his teeth, causing her to draw in her breath sharply with excitement.

Walking behind her again he slid a hand beneath her. She felt him spreading a thick cream over her vulva, covering her inner sex lips and her clitoris before moving upwards, parting her buttocks so that he could spread the lubricant around the entrance to her rectum.

It felt delicious. The moist coolness of the lotion, combined with the sensual movements of his fingers, quickly had her writhing in ecstasy. She felt her body tightening as her climax grew nearer.

'She's going to come,' murmured one of the spectators. The words only increased Natalie's excitement.

'Be careful,' Simon cautioned her softly, but she realised that he knew she couldn't control herself. Her breasts were swollen and throbbing, her flesh consumed with need. Then she felt him up against her and knew that he'd freed himself so that the tip of his erection was nudging against her outer sex lips, sliding smoothly between them as her body sucked him deep inside her. As he moved rapidly in and out, taking care to stimulate her G-spot with every stroke, she felt a heavy pulse throbbing behind her clitoris – and then, without any warning, she climaxed and the delicious hot pulsations of release overwhelmed her.

Simon, who hadn't come, withdrew. When he spoke his voice was cool and detached. 'As you can see,' he said to the excited spectators, 'she failed to control herself. Now, in acknowledgement of her failure to be obedient, she'll ask me to punish her.'

Natalie, who was still being shaken by the occasional final flickers of her orgasm, couldn't believe that this was happening to her. She opened her mouth to speak, to ask for punishment, but the words failed to come. Even now, at this late stage in her training, it was still asking too much of her.

She didn't want to be punished, didn't see why she should be, because all she'd done was allow her sexuality to take over. The pleasure that she'd had was pleasure that Simon had tutored her body to need. It wasn't *her* fault that she'd come, it was *his* – his, and the rules at The Haven.

The room was very quiet. Tension filled the air as everyone waited to see whether or not she would carry out Simon's instructions. 'I'm waiting, Natalie,' said Simon coldly, and she could hear an edge of irritation in his voice.

She still couldn't bring herself to utter the words, to be so completely subjugated to Simon's will, and he put his hand on her lower back. She could feel the tension in his fingers and suddenly understood then that this was as big a test for him as for her. If she didn't do as she was told, if she failed, then Simon had failed too, because her training had been in his hands. For his sake as well as for her own, she had to obey.

'I'm sorry I came,' she whispered. 'Please punish me for not controlling myself better.'

'Believe me, I will,' said Simon. Natalie flinched at the tone of his voice.

The atmosphere in the room was electric as the spectators, along with Natalie, waited to see what her punishment would be. For what seemed an eternity she was left in suspense. Then she heard a tapping sound as something hard touched the beam next to her.

'Can you guess what this is?' asked Simon.

Natalie could. She was certain that it was the handle of a riding crop. Immediately, her body grew tight with fear as Simon's left hand moved over her buttocks and down the backs of her thighs. Then, after a pause that was scarcely endurable, she felt a sharp stinging sensation just beneath the cheeks of her bottom. It wasn't really a pain, but it stung and she squealed as the crop struck again, only this time a fraction higher.

In all the crop rose and fell six times, and never in the same place twice. By the time Simon had flicked the whip for the final time Natalie's skin felt as though it was glowing fiery red. The heat excited her so that she wriggled against the bar, trying to increase the pressure on her belly because her wanton body was looking for pleasure.

Natalie was shocked at herself. How could she have

become so depraved, she wondered. How could anyone find pleasure in humiliation and discomfort? She didn't know the answer, she only knew the truth. Which was that the whole scenario was the most exciting thing that had ever happened to her.

Once the punishment had finished, Simon brought two young women forward from the group of spectators. 'Natalie has always thought that she knew what was best for her body,' he explained. 'And I know from your records that you two believe this as well. If it's true then she should find it almost impossible to resist your attempts to pleasure her.'

'You mean we're to make her come?' asked one of the girls.

'If you can. But, of course, Natalie will try to resist.'

Natalie bit on her lower lip in despair as one of the girls drew the tip of a pointed fingernail around each of Natalie's areolae. 'I know how lovely this feels,' whispered the girl. 'It will make you feel so good. Then, when your nipples are hard, I shall pinch them. It will be perfect – wait and see.'

Her words drove Natalie almost insane with desire because they were so true. As the girl's fingernail delicately touched the rapidly swelling flesh, Natalie felt herself growing damp between her thighs. As soon as her nipples hardened and the girl pinched them, she was pierced by an exquisite sensation of aching pleasure that had her struggling frantically to subdue her rapidly building climax.

It was at this point, just when she was at her most vulnerable, that the other girl managed to position herself so that she was able to open up Natalie's sex lips with her hands. She then caressed the needy, damp flesh with the delicate touch of her tongue.

'No, please!' cried Natalie. 'It feels too good. I know I'm going to come.'

'You should have better control than that by now,' said Simon sternly, and she wished that he was right. She didn't want to come again, didn't want to be punished in front of all these people. But she was so excited that it was impossible to distract herself. As the second girl's tongue swirled lightly on the tip of Natalie's clitoris her whole body went rigid, and she cried out as a climax flooded through her.

The first girl continued caressing and fondling Natalie's breasts until her body was completely still. 'That sounded good,' she murmured. 'Why is it that men can't give us that kind of pleasure?'

Natalie didn't answer because she now knew that the girl was wrong. Some men *could* give her as much pleasure as that – but only if she was willing to let them.

'Another failure,' said Simon heavily. 'You know what to do.'

Natalie wondered how many times this was going to happen. 'I'm so sorry,' she said, her voice almost breaking with despair. 'I tried, truly I did.'

'Not hard enough,' he commented.

This time she didn't have to wait very long to find out what her punishment would be. A few seconds later Simon parted the cheeks of her bottom and she felt the tip of a soft, jelly-like vibrating probe being pressed against the opening to her rectum. Because of the ointment that he'd smoothed on earlier it slid in easily. As it vibrated inside her, arousing her already over-stimulated nerve endings, the initial discomfort quickly passed and her body responded by giving Natalie yet another orgasm. She frantically tried to disguise it, both from Simon and from the spectators.

'It seems you've grown to like being punished,' Simon whispered as he finally withdrew the merciless probe. 'I'm going to climax inside you now, but you're still not to come. Is that understood?'

'Yes.'

As the spectators watched in excited silence, Simon drove into her once more. This time he started with a slow rhythm, sliding gently in and out of her and rotating his hips so that every part of her was stimulated. Her stomach swelled, the pressure from the beam only increasing the tight heaviness inside her belly. She was amazed at how quickly her pleasure began to build again, but determined that this time Simon wouldn't triumph. She *would* control herself, no matter what he did to her.

Gradually the tempo of Simon's thrusts quickened until he was driving in and out of Natalie hard and fast, the front of his hips slamming against her buttocks with every forward movement. Very soon she was perilously close to the point of no return. Realising this, she waited until he was deep inside her, then clenched her pelvic muscles tightly around him, squeezing him in a series of rapid muscular spasms.

She heard the breath catch in his throat, and knew that she was forcing him to climax before he wanted. He struggled to delay his own orgasm, but as she tightened herself around him again she knew that he wouldn't last very much longer. Unfortunately, every time she milked him her own pleasure was heightened. Beads of sweat fell from her forehead to the floor as she grew hot and slippery with need. Suddenly, she felt the first tingles of her climax and knew that she was now past the point of no return. She was about to cry out in despair – but then, with a muffled groan, Simon spilt himself inside her and at last she was safe.

Still afraid of being punished, she waited as long as she could, her body poised at the delicious pinnacle of pleasure. 'You can come now,' said Simon, his voice thick with passion. 'You outlasted me.' As he spoke he reached round in front of her and dug his fingers hard into her right breast. Immediately her third – and most intense – orgasm flooded through her, only this time it was all right. Because this time there would be no punishment.

For several minutes Natalie lay slumped against the beam, her breathing rapid, her muscles limp and exhausted. 'Is that it?' she heard one of the watching men ask.

'I think it is,' said another, in a regretful voice.

'Let's see what's going on in the other rooms, then.'

Within seconds the dark, windowless room was empty except for Natalie and Simon. She felt his hands unfastening the cuffs that were tying her wrists to her ankles and then he was helping her up, massaging her muscles as she tried to straighten her back.

'You're wonderful,' he said quietly. 'Absolutely magnificent.'

'I did it for you,' she replied.

He nodded. 'I know.'

'You *do* feel something for me, don't you?' asked Natalie.

'It isn't allowed,' said Simon slowly.

'That's not what I asked you.'

'Perhaps I do. But there's nothing we can do about it. I don't want to lose my job here.'

'Not even if you get a good job in journalism?' she asked.

'I don't think I want to know what you mean by that,' said Simon. 'I'll take you upstairs now – unless you want to look at some of the other things that are going on down here?'

'I don't need to,' said Natalie. 'I think I've learned everything that I needed to from my two weekends at The Haven. What I really want to do is shower and rest.'

'That sounds like a good idea,' agreed Simon. 'I tell

you what, I'll bring you something to eat in about an hour. You didn't have breakfast, remember?'

'That would be nice,' said Natalie, managing to keep the excitement out of her voice. It was now clear to her that Simon was as attracted to her as she was to him. What wasn't clear was how their relationship could progress. Because her stay was nearly over.

Chapter Sixteen

'Delicious!' exclaimed Natalie, after *she'd* wolfed down the ham salad and drunk the glass of wine that Simon had brought her.

'I would have brought you more. But I knew you wouldn't want to be too full, because of this afternoon.'

Natalie frowned. 'What do you mean?'

'I thought you knew what happened on your final afternoon here,' said Simon. 'Rob Gill likes to see for himself how much his clients have benefited from the course, no matter who their tutor is. He and Sue will devote themselves to pleasuring you. The important thing is that you remember not to take the initiative at any point. He simply wants to make sure that you no longer try and keep control during sex.'

'Will you be there?'

'I'll be watching, but I'm not allowed to join in. It's the time when I evaluate your progress, for my notes.'

'I see,' said Natalie slowly. She didn't know whether to be pleased or not. In a way she was excited, because it would be yet another new experience for her. On the other hand, she was no longer really interested in anyone but Simon. However, in order to complete the course satisfactorily, and get the list of members, Rob Gill would have to be content with her progress. Clearly this was the only way in which he could truly test it.

A short time later she accompanied Simon to a small lounge at the back of the house. The door had a notice reading 'Staff Only' on it and there, waiting for her in the middle of the room, was Rob Gill.

He smiled at her, his piercing blue eyes approving. 'I watched you this morning. You've come a long way,' he congratulated her.

'Yes, thanks to Simon and your programme.'

'Would you consider yourself a satisfied customer?'

Natalie nodded. 'I certainly would.'

'That's excellent news. Sue and I are going to ensure that you're satisfied in every way before you actually leave here. From this moment give yourself over to me. Together with Sue, I'll take the responsibility for your pleasure. I'm sure you won't fail your tutor now. I know how much Simon means to you.'

A warning note sounded in Natalie's brain. 'He's certainly been a good tutor,' she agreed.

Rob didn't answer. 'Sue, would you undress Natalie, please?'

Natalie stood tall and straight as the auburn-haired girl, whom she'd first met at the reception desk the previous week, unzipped the back of her dress and then eased it off over her shoulders. Beneath it Natalie was wearing a cream lacy bra and cream-edged panties, but no stockings. 'You have lovely breasts,' murmured Sue, and for a few seconds she sucked lightly at Natalie's nipples through the lacy material. Natalie felt the flesh between her thighs tingle in excited anticipation as the fabric caressed her swiftly hardening nipples. Then Sue stopped sucking and removed the bra.

As she pulled Natalie's panties down she kissed the blonde girl's lower belly and licked at the skin over her hip bones, causing them to jerk. Natalie thrust her pelvis forward in an uncontrollable movement. 'Don't be in such a hurry,' whispered Sue. 'The pleasure will start soon enough.'

Now completely naked, Natalie waited and watched as Rob advanced towards her, a blindfold in his hand. She wished that she didn't have to wear it, because she'd wanted to watch what they were doing. But again she knew that she had no choice. It was up to Rob how her pleasure was granted to her.

Once her eyes were covered, he and Sue carefully laid her on the carpet. Then, to her surprise, she heard the soft murmur of voices. Now fresh hands were holding her wrists and ankles, spreadeagling her body and opening her up for Rob and Sue. She wondered who they were, and where they'd been waiting. Luckily she had very little time to reflect on this because, almost immediately, Sue's small fingers were fondling her breasts. Then the auburn-haired girl began to use her mouth again on Natalie's aching nipples, causing her to utter tiny cries of pleasure.

She was expecting to feel Rob's hands on her next, but instead another small pair of hands started to cover her body with oil. It was only then that she realised she'd been tricked. Rob and Sue were not going to pleasure her on their own. There were other people in the room with them, other people who were going to touch and arouse her. Surprisingly, she no longer cared because already someone was sucking on her toes as their fingers caressed her ankles, while yet another person turned her on her side so that she could be aroused in many different ways.

They worked slowly and gently at first, caressing her flesh, stroking it with silk scarves and feathers until her body would spasm and ripple in climax. Then they would leave her for a few moments before re-arousing her, softly and carefully bringing her to one orgasm after another. She'd never felt so pampered, so relaxed. But then, when her flesh started to fail to respond to the gentle stimuli, the tempo changed.

Natalie thought that the women had withdrawn because all the hands felt larger, harder. Now, as she lay on her left side with her right leg over her left, someone parted the cheeks of her bottom. A finger tickled the entrance to her rectum before allowing some drops of oil to spill on to it. Her flesh flinched at the unexpected cool touch of the liquid. But, before she'd had time to recover, a large, thick vibrator was being inserted into her back passage and immediately it was switched on.

Her body began to shake. She cried out with a mixture of pain and pleasure, and her breasts were squashed against a man's chest. Then she felt hands parting her sex lips and the tip of a penis was sliding up and down her inner channel. Every time it glided over her swollen, throbbing clitoris she gasped with delight.

Her entire being was suffused with incredible sensations. The speed of the vibrator was increased, and at the same time the man – possibly Rob, she thought – who was lying against her slid himself into her so that she was completely and utterly full.

Natalie could feel her whole body shaking. As the tension built she wondered how her over-stimulated system was going to cope when she finally climaxed. It wasn't long before she knew the answer. As her nerve endings went frantic with pleasure, and her breasts began to become engorged, her muscles started to contract. A climax tore through her, causing her body to spasm as though she'd been electrocuted.

She jerked back and forth, and every movement caused further stimulation as the vibrator continued its remorseless work and the man, his erection inserted deeply within her, thrust strongly. She could hear herself making strange crying sounds as, half delirious with pleasure, she allowed these strangers to have their way with her.

After that Natalie lost count of how many times she came, or exactly what they did to her. Some of the women returned. They carefully licked and sucked at her shrinking clitoris until she came again while their small, supple fingers worked their magic inside her. They pressed against the walls of her vagina, rubbing gently over her G-spot until the sweet ache suffused her entire belly and she cramped in yet another spasm of release.

She lost all sense of time, and all sense of reality. The only things that mattered were the pleasure she was being given and the wonderful feeling that she had of being able, at long last, to abandon herself utterly to the desires of other people so as to obtain such an incredible reward.

Eventually Rob spoke. 'That's enough,' he said – and, to her everlasting shame, she cried out, because she didn't want it to end. But everyone obeyed him instantly, and abruptly she was left alone, her hot, sweat-streaked flesh still trembling slightly in the aftermath of the sexual excesses of the afternoon.

There was no longer anyone holding her wrists and ankles but she felt too exhausted to move. Every muscle seemed limp: it felt as though her bones had turned to liquid and she was completely weightless. It was an extraordinary feeling, and one that she suspected she would never experience again.

'You've certainly gained a lot from our course,' said Rob, removing the blindfold. 'Your tutor is to be congratulated.'

Natalie, still breathless, nodded. 'I don't feel I wasted my money.'

Rob smiled. 'No, that was self-evident. You can leave whenever you like now. There are no more lessons, I'm afraid, because you don't need them. As for my talk, I think you can skip it. You understand our rules. I'd say you're one of the most receptive clients we've ever had. What do you think, Simon?'

'I've seen better,' said Simon laconically.

Rob's eyes narrowed. 'Are you sure?'

'Yes.'

'Good. I wouldn't like either of you to forget that this is a course, and that there must be no personal feelings between tutors and clients. In case either of you have forgotten, it's even more important that Natalie leaves straight away.'

'I can't be answerable for Natalie but I'd have thought you knew *me* well enough to be certain I understood the rules,' said Simon sharply.

Natalie realised that she should say something, anything at all in order to stop Rob's suspicions. 'I know the course has changed me,' she said, as she sat up and started to look for her clothes. 'It hasn't made me a different person, though, and Simon really isn't my type.'

'I'm glad to hear it,' said Rob. He held out his hand. 'I hope that we'll see you back here at some of our annual reunions. They're more like two-day parties, run over Christmas and Easter and times like that. They aren't really lessons, they're simply gatherings of people who know how to enjoy themselves, if you understand me.'

'I understand you, and I'd love to come,' said Natalie, with a smile.

Rob left the room and Natalie opened her mouth to speak. But Simon flicked his eyes warningly towards the corner of the room, and she guessed that they were probably still being filmed. 'You can go now,' she said crisply to him. 'I'll put my clothes on, get packed and leave.'

'I'll take your bags to the car when you're ready,' said Simon. But he managed to sound totally uninterested in her and Natalie hoped that between them they'd thrown Rob off the scent.

By the time Simon came up to her room to collect her bags, Natalie had changed into a light beige linen suit, its long-line jacket draped over a lilac camisole top.

'I see you've got your businesswoman's armour on again,' he remarked.

She didn't like to say that this was because she was trying to forget what had happened downstairs. Somehow she needed to regain control of her life, to rediscover her business persona and – ridiculous as it seemed – the clothes helped. 'It's comfortable for travelling in,' she replied.

He gave a half-smile. 'Of course. How silly of me to think otherwise. Here, let me carry those.'

In silence they walked out of the room. Natalie glanced back once, and she had a momentary vision of herself balanced over the bar, her fingers clasping her ankles. But she turned away immediately, knowing that it was time to put all that behind her.

Simon didn't speak until they were crossing the car park. 'I hope you have a good journey.'

Natalie looked at him in surprise. 'Is that all you've got to say?'

'I think so.'

'You look cross. What's the matter?'

'Nothing.' He looked briefly at her but then glanced away again, unable to maintain eye contact.

'You didn't like what happened to me earlier, did you?' asked Natalie.

'I didn't mind. I've seen it all before. It goes with the territory.'

'But it upset you, didn't it?'

'No.'

'I don't believe you.'

'It doesn't matter whether you believe me or not.'

'But it does,' said Natalie, catching hold of the sleeve of his jacket. 'It matters to both of us. You know that as well as I do.'

'Be careful,' said Simon quietly. 'Even here it's possible that we're being filmed.'

'Tell me the truth. Did you mind having to watch?'

'Yes,' he admitted reluctantly. 'I minded a lot. I wanted it to be me inside you, me plunging the vibrator into your rectum, me doing all those things that gave you such pleasure.'

'You were jealous, then?' She couldn't keep the delight out of her voice.

'That pleases you, doesn't it?'

'Only because I care.'

He sighed heavily. 'It's irrelevant whether you care or not. I'm not going to risk losing this job and we're never likely to meet again.'

'But we could,' she said excitedly.

'How?'

'You could come and work for me.'

Simon looked at her incredulously and then laughed. 'You have *got* to be joking!'

'Why?'

'Do you really think, feeling the way that I do about you, that I'd be willing to sit in an office and take orders from you all day? I don't think that would do much for our sex life.'

'Why not? I think it would be exciting. We'd both know that it was a charade, and that once we were alone together you'd be the one in charge.'

'I'm not sure you'd be able to play that kind of game,' said Simon. 'If the truth be told, lots of our clients regress after they've been here. In a few months' time you'll want control in every aspect of your life again, including the bedroom.'

'I won't!'

'It wouldn't work.'

'We'll never know unless we try. Look, I'm already going to use that piece that you brought me. If you do want to take me up on my offer, then there'll be a job vacancy starting in four weeks' time. That's the last Monday in June. I won't advertise it and you needn't make up your mind until the last moment.'

She could tell that he was tempted. But she also knew how difficult it would be for him to take orders from her all day, no matter how much in control he was at night. For her the prospect was incredibly exciting, but for him she guessed that it seemed demeaning. 'I'd never really be your boss,' she continued hastily. 'It would all be a game.'

'No, it wouldn't. It's your magazine. Of course you'd be in charge at work.'

'But it's a way for us to get together again. If it didn't work out in the office then you could look for another job, but at least having had a position on my magazine you'd stand a better chance of getting a good job elsewhere. Being freelance hasn't exactly opened all the doors for you.'

'That's precisely the kind of remark that puts me off the idea,' said Simon coldly.

'Please think about it,' she begged him.

There was a long pause. 'I'll let you know,' agreed Simon at last. 'Now, here's a list of members whom you can contact whenever you like.'

'For what?'

'Use your imagination. Surely *that*'s improved while you've been here. Ex-clients usually throw dinners for each other, or parties at weekends. Your friend Jan Pearson has had a lot of fun since she spent a weekend with us. Now you'll be able to join in her parties too. Isn't that what brought you here, the fact that she'd shut you out of her life?'

Natalie nodded. 'Yes, it is. I'd forgotten, it seems such a long time ago.'

'It *was* a long time ago, and you were a very different person then.'

'It's you who changed me,' whispered Natalie. 'You can't abandon me now. You've taught me to enjoy dark pleasures, things that I never knew existed. I can't go back to my old ways. What will become of me if we don't meet again?'

'I've already told you, that's what this list is for. It enables you to explore your new-found sexuality with people of similar tastes.'

'But it's *you* I want.'

'I'm very flattered to hear it,' said Simon, starting to turn away.

'Wait!' called Natalie. 'What about the job?'

'I've told you, I'll think about it. Don't hold your breath, though.' With that he walked away.

Natalie climbed into the car. She knew that she should feel elated. She'd had a wonderful weekend, done incredible things and received fantastic pleasure. But none of that counted for anything if she was never going to see Simon again.

If he hadn't been jealous that afternoon then she wouldn't have been quite so certain that he needed her as badly as she needed him. However, since he'd admitted to it, she knew for certain that they were meant to be together. Ironically, all that she'd learned would count for very little if, because she was still going to be in control at work, she lost the first man she'd ever met who seemed like a soulmate. A man who could play her body like no man she'd ever met before – or was ever likely to meet again.

'What are you doing this weekend, Natalie?' asked Grace, as Natalie prepared to leave the office nearly two weeks after her last visit to The Haven.

'I'm spending the weekend with a friend, Jan Pearson. You probably remember her, she's a freelance casting director.'

'Oh, yes. You and she used to see a lot of each other.'

'Yes, well, she's been very busy but she's back in circulation now.'

'Have a good time, then.'

'Thanks,' said Natalie. 'I'm sure I will.'

Once she got home she threw a few personal items into a small overnight bag and then drove to Jan's. She was looking forward to the weekend because it was the first party for ex-visitors to The Haven that she'd been to. But there was one drawback. Simon wasn't going to be there.

'Hi!' enthused Jan as she opened her front door. 'Long time no see. God, you look well. Did you enjoy your stay at The Haven?' she added, with a wicked laugh.

'I had two weekends there,' Natalie reminded her. 'They were brilliant.'

'Good. You should enjoy yourself this weekend. You may know some of the people.'

'Where am I sleeping?' asked Natalie.

'You'll probably have a better idea of that after dinner,' replied Jan. 'Come through, we're just about to sit down to eat.'

Natalie didn't recognise anyone sitting round the table, but as the evening progressed she began to feel excitement building within her. She was particularly attracted to the man on her left, whose dark brown hair was quite long and whose eyes reminded her a little of Simon's. 'What's your speciality?' he asked, as they were drinking coffee.

'My magazine caters for single businesswomen,' replied Natalie.

He looked surprised and then laughed. 'That's not quite what I meant. I was referring to your sexual taste.'

'Oh, I see. I'm sorry, I'm afraid half my mind's still at the office.'

'Well, we can't have that. So, what do you like?'

She felt her stomach tighten and there was an aching

heaviness between her thighs. 'I like to be dominated,' she confessed in a low voice.

'Good. How about we get to know each other a little better?'

'That sounds like a good idea.'

'You won't mind if my friend joins us, will you?' he added. Now Natalie's heart was thudding against her ribs as a fair-haired man also got up from the table. The three of them headed towards the stairs.

'Have a nice time,' called Jan, busy chatting to a tall, heavy-set man who looked more dangerous than Natalie would have cared to risk trying. Jan had said that his name was Richard, and that they'd met at The Haven.

Once upstairs it was obvious that the two men had been there before, because they immediately led her into a small room. Then, before she had time to catch her breath, the dark-haired one, whose name was William, was stripping off her clothes while his friend opened a drawer and drew out a leather outfit which the pair of them then put on her. Within a few minutes Natalie had a studded leather collar round her neck, cuffs on her wrists and ankles, a tight-fitting black leather bra with cut-out holes for her nipples and crotchless black leather panties that they pulled tight so that immediately the pressure deep within her was heightened.

The blond man lay on the bed, his erection already huge. 'Use your mouth on that,' said William. 'And at the same time he'll use his mouth on you. Do you want to come or not?' he asked his friend casually.

'Yes, I think so.'

William turned to Natalie. 'Right, so use your mouth on him until he comes. The longer you can make him last the better for you, I guess. I'll just watch: it will be my turn next.'

Natalie was surprised at how frightened she felt. It wasn't that either of them were threatening her, but the outfit made her feel enslaved, subservient, and there was no one else there to control the situation even though downstairs the party was in full swing.

She hesitated, but then realised that the fear had only increased her desire. She desperately wanted to feel the blond man's tongue snaking through her crotchless black leather panties, plunging deep within her and caressing her swollen, aching clitoris.

'Is something the matter?' asked William. He sounded slightly irritated.

'Of course not,' said Natalie hastily. 'I'm sorry,' she added, and immediately William smiled. As Natalie positioned herself so that her vulva was over the blond man's mouth and her own mouth over his straining erection she felt herself trembling with the kind of excitement that she'd previously only known at The Haven.

'Off you go, then,' said William. 'If things don't look to be going too well, I can always lend a hand.'

Natalie didn't know what he meant, and she didn't care because now her mouth was closing hungrily around the blond man's swollen member. Because Natalie was on top of him he was in the perfect position to give her exquisite pleasure. It was quickly apparent to her that he was an expert at satisfying women in this way. He stroked his tongue gently upwards against the shaft of her clitoris, which produced the most delicious sensations. As she held his penis in one hand and began to lick its sides, so he flicked his tongue inside her vagina for a few seconds before moving the tip of his tongue first against one side of her throbbing nub of pleasure and then against the other.

Very soon her body trembled with her first orgasm of

the evening and momentarily she lost her rhythm, forgetting that she was meant to continue pleasuring the man beneath her. She was soon reminded. William tugged on her leather collar, then flicked his fingers hard against the sensitive skin at the curve of her waist, causing her to jerk with surprise. A burning, stinging sensation spread through her. 'You're forgetting my friend,' he said commandingly. Immediately she was reminded of Simon, and the way he'd instructed her at The Haven.

'I'm sorry,' Natalie mumbled and then continued stimulating the blond man. Now she flicked her tongue over the underside of his straining erection and his hips twitched with pleasure. In return, he twirled the tip of his tongue very lightly on top of her clitoris. She was immediately flooded with glorious, intense spasms of hot pulsating pleasure that caused her to climax yet again.

Once more she lost her rhythm and this time she felt a stinging blow across her buttocks, just above the line of her tight leather pants – a blow that couldn't have come simply from William's fingers. However, she didn't dare turn her head to see what he'd struck her with because her concentration was now focused on his friend. Despite this, the blond man succeeded in giving her two more orgasms before he himself finally climaxed. His hips pumped as he spilled himself into her mouth, and she sucked greedily on the delicious, viscous hot fluid that spilled out of him.

Immediately he'd finished, the blond man rolled out from beneath Natalie. Now William pushed her roughly on to her back, spreading her arms high above her head as he covered her body with his. Lowering his mouth to her breasts, he used his tongue and teeth on her nipples where they protruded through the opening in the bra, until she was squirming with frantic desire. Then he thrust savagely into her and, although he didn't bother to stimulate her in any other way, because the coupling was so swift and urgent her body responded with yet another climax and she gave a wild cry of pleasure.

It was only when it was over and William got off her that Natalie felt that something was wrong. 'Great!' he enthused. 'See you around, I hope.'

'Yes, of course,' she murmured and the blond man, who had never told her his name, smiled back. Then both men left her. She was still clad in the leather outfit and wearing a collar of subservience. Once they'd gone

Natalie felt very lonely. It wasn't that she hadn't enjoyed the sex – she had – but she wished that one of them had stayed with her even if it was only to help her undress. Now that the pleasure was over she felt empty and lost.

Taking off the leather outfit, she looked in the next-door bedroom. There she saw a girl tied to the bed while three men had their way with her. The girl was blindfolded and completely helpless, whimpering in frustration as the men played with her, remorselessly toying with her and denying her satisfaction in the same way that the course at The Haven had denied it to Natalie.

She was excited by the sight of the other girl's taut, moist body but it only made her miss Simon all the more. Suddenly she didn't want to stay at the party any longer. Physically the activities suited her, but mentally it wasn't enough. She realised that she needed more – more than simply sexual pleasure. The truth was, she needed Simon too.

She dressed quickly and then went quietly downstairs, taking her overnight bag with her. Jan was coming up the stairs with Richard. 'You're not leaving already, are you?' she asked in surprise. 'The party's only just begun.'

'I had a call on my mobile,' lied Natalie. 'I'm needed at the office tomorrow.'

'Oh no!' Jan pulled a face. 'That's really rotten luck. I hope you had a good time with William and Lance.'

'Lance, is that his name?'

'He's the blond man, yes.'

'Well, I suppose it's nice to know, even if it is a little late.'

'Names don't matter,' laughed Jan. 'It's the action that counts. I'll call you later in the week.'

'I look forward to it,' said Natalie. Then she let herself out into the night.

As she drove away she couldn't help wondering what was going to become of her if she never saw Simon again and spent the rest of her life at parties like these. Parties where her keenly honed body could receive the kind of satisfaction it needed but where, she now knew, she would always be left with a sense of something missing.

Chapter Seventeen

Eventually it was the the last Monday in June when, if he was going to accept her invitation, Simon would arrive at the office. Natalie got up in the morning with a feeling of excited anticipation. She looked through her wardrobe with extra care, wondering what she should wear that would look both efficient and attractive. Then, realising what she was doing, she took out the dark blue suit and cream blouse that was almost her work uniform.

'I'm not going to start changing just for you, Simon Ellis,' she muttered to herself. 'At work you'll have to accept me as I am.'

When she got to the office she asked Grace if there'd been any calls for her, but there hadn't. Disappointed, Natalie settled herself behind her desk and tried to concentrate on work. She had a meeting at ten and when she left for it there was no sign of Simon. When she returned at twelve-thirty he still hadn't shown up, and now she began to feel depressed. She'd felt so sure that he would have been missing her that she couldn't believe he wasn't going to come.

Afraid of missing him she even delayed her lunch, but at one-thirty she decided that she was being completely ridiculous. Clearly she'd been wrong about everything, and somehow she would have to learn to live with that. 'I'm going out to lunch,' she told Grace. 'I'll be about an hour.'

'Simon Ellis has arrived,' replied her secretary. 'Shall I ask him to come back later?'

'No!' said Natalie loudly, and then she checked herself. 'I mean, that's okay. Show him through. I'm not that hungry, anyway.'

When Simon walked through the door Natalie felt a fluttering sensation in her solar plexus and her heart began to race. If anything, he was even more attractive than she'd remembered. His dark eyes gleamed in his pale, strong-boned face. 'Sorry I'm late,' he said coolly. 'The car broke down.'

'Not a very good start,' responded Natalie.

'No,' he agreed. 'I read my article in your magazine last month. You hadn't changed a word.'

'I've better things to do than change my contributors' words. If they're not good enough to write a decent article then I don't employ them.'

Simon nodded. 'That makes sense. So, is this position that you mentioned still open?'

'Yes. My secretary will explain it to you, but on the whole you'll be doing similar articles to the one of yours we've already published. Most months you can choose the subject. Occasionally, particularly if it's a themed issue, then I'll have to decide. The content will always be yours. Right now I need a nine-hundred-word piece on pets as substitutes for men in the lives of single career women. Do you think you could do that for me?'

Simon raised his eyebrows. 'I'm not a pet person.'

'Neither am I,' said Natalie briskly. 'However, you don't need to be a pet lover. Actually, the fact that you aren't one will probably give the article an extra edge. I'd like it on my desk by five-thirty tonight, please.'

Simon got to his feet. 'Of course. What happens when we leave here, Natalie?'

'I thought we'd already discussed that.'

'But are we going back to my place or yours?'

'Mine,' said Natalie quickly.

'I suppose that makes you feel safer, does it, knowing that you can throw me out at any time?'

'It seems a sensible precaution at the start of a relationship.'

'You know, listening to you talk like that makes me wonder whether The Haven changed you at all,' said Simon.

'I don't wish to discuss The Haven during office hours.'

'I'm sure you don't. Just make sure that you don't forget it when the office door closes behind you at night.'

Once he'd left her office Natalie realised how tense she was. Her shoulders were up round her ears, and she took a few deep breaths and massaged her scalp in order to free some of the tension. Simon's incredible sexuality, his raw animal magnetism, was so great that it had been very difficult for her to concentrate on work. She'd also been afraid that he'd try to undermine her authority in some way, and was relieved that he hadn't. The only thing was, as she was going to keep her guard up all day she wasn't certain how easy it would be to let it down at night.

At five o'clock, Simon walked back into her office and placed some sheets of paper in front of her. 'There you are, the article you asked for. I've met the deadline with half an hour to spare.'

Natalie nodded. 'Very commendable. That gives me time to go through it before we leave.'

'As long as you don't try and discuss it once we get home.'

'Back at *my* home, you mean.'

'Oh, Natalie,' said Simon softly. 'When will you learn? I thought it was going to be *our* home, at least for the moment.'

Natalie felt flustered. 'Yes, of course it is, but ...'

'But you still think of it as yours, like this magazine, is that it?'

'No,' she protested. But she knew that he was right. It was going to be very difficult for her to hand over her private life to someone else and by reminding him that the flat they'd be living in would be hers she was attempting to prevent him from taking total control. 'I'll buzz you when I've read this,' she said dismissively.

Twenty minutes later Simon was back in the office. 'Was it all right?' he asked politely.

Natalie frowned. 'I'm afraid not.'

'What's wrong with it?'

'Sit down and I'll tell you.'

For a moment he hesitated. But then, very slowly, he settled himself on the chair opposite her, crossed his arms over his chest and looked thoughtfully at her. 'Fire away.'

'You're patronising our readers,' said Natalie. 'In fact, you've come dangerously close to showing contempt for them. That's not what our magazine's about. The truth is that pets don't judge you by who you are or what you do, they judge you by your actions towards them. *That*'s why career women find their pets better company than men. You make it sound as though there's something wrong with the women.'

'Instead of with the men, you mean?'

'Yes, I suppose so.'

'I don't think there *is* anything wrong with most men. I think that if women want a tame puppy or kitten that's fine. But they can't expect men to behave in the same way.'

Natalie tried to be patient. 'Simon, this isn't about what *you* think, it's about the big picture. It's yet another indication of how successful career women are losing out.'

'Never mind, their loss is the animal kingdom's gain.'

'Don't be flippant. I'd like this redone tomorrow. I know you can do better.'

'Then you know more than I do. Since you seem to have such a good grasp of how the article should be written, perhaps you'd care to do it yourself.'

Natalie began to lose her temper. 'I am the editor, Simon. I have the final say and I say that this isn't good enough. I'm not trying to censor what you write—'

'Yes, you are.'

'I am *not*. I'm simply asking that you take a slightly more sympathetic look at the situation, have a rethink, and then write it again.'

'I didn't realise that censorship flourished under your editorship.'

'It doesn't,' said Natalie, struggling to keep her voice calm. 'The trouble with you is you've been freelance too long and although you've had individual articles accepted you've never had to produce regular features to fit someone else's criteria. I'm sure you'll get the hang of it quite quickly.'

A pale pink colour stained Simon's cheekbones. 'How very kind of you to say so. Why don't you write

"Must try harder" in the margin, just to make sure that I get the message?'

'Don't be childish,' snapped Natalie. 'Here.' She pushed his article across the table towards him.

Simon opened his mouth as though to say more but then closed it again, grabbed the offending article and stalked out of the room.

Natalie slumped in her seat. She knew that she'd been hard on him, harder than she need have been. But she felt that it had been important he understood from the very beginning that at work her word was law.

When Natalie arrived back home Simon was already sitting outside in his car. 'How did you know the way?' she asked.

'I'm quite good with street maps.'

She glanced inside the car. 'You haven't brought much with you.'

'I may not be staying long. I've brought enough for a few nights.'

It felt strange, walking into her flat at the end of the day accompanied by a man who was going to stay for the whole evening and night. She felt an unexpected surge of resentment that he'd now probably expect her to start cooking a meal.

'I always have a glass of wine when I get in,' she said defiantly.

'Fine. I'll have a cold beer.'

'I don't have any beer in.'

'You'd better pick some up on your way to work tomorrow.'

'Pick it up yourself,' retorted Natalie.

Simon grabbed her by the shoulders and pushed her against the kitchen door, his hand pinioning her shoulders against the wood. 'You're not at work now, so you can stop giving orders.'

'*You* gave *me* an order.'

'Yes, but that's because we're at home. The rules change then, remember?'

'This isn't The Haven. The only rules we have to abide by here are mine. It's my home.' The moment the words were out of her mouth she regretted them. Simon's eyes, which had been gleaming, flicked away from her and his hands started to release her shoulders. 'I knew this wouldn't work,' he muttered.

Realising what she'd done, Natalie caught hold of his jacket. 'I'm sorry. This is really difficult for me but I want it to work. I've done nothing but think about you since we last met. I've used the list you gave me to go to parties and dinners, but although they were fun it wasn't the same without you. Please, give me another chance.'

'This has to work for both of us,' said Simon and now his voice was gentle. 'It has to be fun, a way of life that we both enjoy.'

'You didn't look as though you were enjoying yourself in the office.'

'You really have got a sharp tongue haven't you? You know, your problem is that you don't relax enough.' With that, he pushed her against the door once more. Only this time he then kneeled in front of her, pushed her skirt up to her waist, pulled down her panties and closed his mouth around her vulva. Gently he opened her up with his hands so that his tongue could caress her throbbing sex.

Natalie's legs began to shake and she could feel her clitoris tingling as the pleasure grew. Her head fell back against the door as she let the delicious sensations wash over her and then, very quickly, she shook as a wonderfully warm, gentle climax rippled through her.

Simon got to his feet, went to the fridge and poured her a glass of wine. 'Here, you'd better drink this before you start preparing our meal.'

'I don't usually cook,' she confessed.

'You've got pasta, haven't you? That's hardly in Delia Smith's league but it's better than a takeaway. Anyway, I want you to put on some sexy underwear before you start cooking. That should add a little something to the meal.'

'I can't do that,' protested Natalie.

'Why not? It's what I want.'

Natalie was becoming very excited. Although a part of her resented what was happening another part of her found it very arousing. When she was in her bedroom changing into a black lacy underwired bra and matching lace panties she caressed her body with her hands, glancing at herself in the full-length mirror as she did so. The length of her legs was emphasised by the high heels that she put on to go with the black lace-topped hold-up stockings. Her body was so desperate for a caress that she fondled her own nipples for a moment before returning, with rather flushed cheeks, to the kitchen.

All the time she cooked the meal Simon was touching her. He ran his fingers down the curve of her spine, put his hands on each side of her waist and pressed inwards so that she longed for them to move lower down. Then he released her and contented himself with nuzzling the nape of her neck. It was incredibly difficult for her to concentrate on the pasta and by the time they sat down to eat it wasn't food that she was hungry for – it was Simon.

'Delicious,' he remarked as he ate the tagliatelle. 'You make a very sexy cook.'

'I *feel* very sexy,' she confessed.

Simon smiled. 'That's good, because I've got a little surprise prepared for later.'

After that Natalie completely lost her appetite because all she could think about was what he might be going to do to her, and how much her body would enjoy the pleasure that she was finally going to be allowed to receive.

When they were finishing their coffee the doorbell rang. 'Oh no,' groaned Natalie. 'Who could it be? No one ever calls on me at this time of the evening. I won't bother answering it.'

'You have to answer it,' said Simon firmly.

'I can't, not dressed like this.'

'Yes, you can. Go and answer the door. Now,' he added.

Natalie stared at him. 'But what will they think?'

'I don't care what they think. I want you to do it. I want to know that you're standing there dressed like that, looking so sexy and provocative.'

Just as she had at The Haven, Natalie began to feel vulnerable and humiliated. But clearly this was what she needed because her nipples hardened into tiny rigid points and the touch of her lacy bra against them sent electric shocks darting through her breasts. Obediently she got to her feet and went to the front door. There she hesitated for a moment, her heart racing. Then, knowing that Simon would soon start getting annoyed, she forced herself to open the door.

To her incredulous delight, standing in the doorway were Sajel and Anil. 'I've been trying to ring you ever since my second weekend at The Haven!' she said. 'I had your number but there was never any answer.'

'We've been away, getting reacquainted,' explained Sajel, with a demure smile.

'You look very nice, and I'm sure your neighbours appreciate it but perhaps we could come in?' suggested Anil.

'Oh God, I forgot,' cried Natalie, and she quickly stood back to let them in. 'Simon's staying for a few days,' she explained.

'We know,' said Anil. 'He was the one who asked us to come over. He wanted tonight to be special for you.'

Natalie's chest felt tight with excitement. 'You mean, you've come to join us?'

'Of course,' said Sajel. 'It will be fun, won't it?'

'Oh, yes,' agreed Natalie.

'There, what do you think of my surprise?' asked Simon, as the three of them joined him in the small dining-kitchen.

'I can't think of anything you could have done that would have pleased me more,' admitted Natalie.

'Good. Well, I think we've finished with the coffee so I suggest we all have a drink and then go upstairs.'

As the four of them entered Natalie's bedroom she and Sajel glanced at each other. 'It's like being back at The Haven, isn't it?' whispered the Indian girl.

'Even better than that,' replied Natalie. 'Now we're doing what we want – and with the men we've chosen.'

'Right, girls,' said Simon. 'We're going to play a game. Once you're undressed Anil is going to give each of you a massage, so that both of you are in the mood for what will follow.

Once he's done that I shall dress you in something a little special, then Anil will try and bring Sajel to a climax while I do the same with Natalie. The idea is for Anil and me to try our very best to make you come, but for you to delay your pleasure as long as you can. The winner will be the girl who controls herself best.'

'Is there a prize?' asked Sajel.

Simon smiled. 'Only a punishment, I'm afraid.'

With rising excitement the two girls stripped off their clothes and then took it in turns to lie on Natalie's king-sized bed while Anil covered them with perfumed massage oil. He worked on Sajel first. As Natalie listened to the other girl's sighs of pleasure her own breathing quickened, and she felt her excitement growing. 'Enjoying yourself?' whispered Simon in her ear. She didn't answer. She didn't have to, because her trembling flesh told him all he needed to know.

At last it was her turn. As she lay face down on the bed and felt Anil's strong fingers kneading the muscles in her shoulders and neck, before travelling lower down the sides of her spine and over her buttocks, she gave a low moan of pleasure. She'd forgotten how clever his fingers were, and was surprised at how skilfully his massage both relaxed and aroused her.

When he'd finished with her back Anil rolled her over, and she stared up at him unblinking as his fingers skimmed lightly over the delicate bones of her shoulders before massaging her tight little breasts. He took particular care to oil her highly sensitive nipples, and she felt them start to throb and ache. Before his hands moved lower down her body he brushed the palms against the rigid tips and, to her shame, she nearly came then. It took a supreme effort for her to control herself.

While Anil continued to work on Natalie's lower body, although he took care to avoid the area between her thighs she wondered how on earth she was going to stop her pleasure from erupting immediately Simon began to arouse her.

'There, that's done,' said Anil when he'd finished sliding his fingers over her feet and between her toes, which was incredibly sensual. 'Do we want them to lie side by side while we work on them, Simon?'

'I think so,' agreed Simon. 'It will add to their excitement if they can hear each other's responses. First, though, I have to put the silk on them.'

Natalie sat up on the bed and watched as Simon fastened a thick leather belt tightly around Sajel's small waist. At the front and back of the belt there were round metal rings. She watched as he took hold of a long, narrow strip of silk, got Sajel to stand in front of him with her legs apart and then fastened one end of the silk in the ring at the back of her before passing the material between her legs and up through the ring at the front, giving it a firm tug to make sure that it was tight.

Sajel uttered a little squeal and Natalie wondered what it felt like. 'That's all I'm going to do,' said Simon. 'Your turn, Natalie.'

Sajel stood to one side. Natalie stood passively in front of her lover as he fastened a similar belt around her waist, cinching it tightly, and then she felt the caress of the silken material between her thighs. Anil's massage had aroused her so much that she was already very damp. Because the strip of material was narrow it slid between her outer sex lips, pressing firmly against the inner, throbbing flesh and her hard, aching clitoris. Now, with the added pressure of the material, her lower belly felt tight and her thighs started to tremble.

Quickly the two girls were laid side by side on their backs and ordered to close their eyes. Then Natalie waited, hardly daring to breathe until she felt the two men get on to the bed. In her mind she'd imagined many things that might happen to her, but she was completely taken by surprise when she felt the soft caress of what seemed to be a tiny pointed brush moving over the silk. This would have been stimulating enough on its own, but the brush was wet and cool, which meant that the more Simon drew it back and forth over the tight silk that was cutting into her sex the more her nerve endings leaped and tightened.

Soon Natalie could hear herself moaning with ecstasy while next to her Sajel moved restlessly on the bed, muttering incoherently and occasionally uttering cries of desperation. Natalie recognised that these were caused because the Indian girl was close to coming.

The atmosphere in the room was electric. Both the men were so knowledgeable about their partners' reactions, so clever at bringing them to the point of no return, that it was sweet agony for both of the girls to have to try to control their natural responses. After a time Natalie felt that she was going to explode. 'Does it feel good?' whispered Simon. 'I know you want to come, but you mustn't let me down. It isn't just that I don't want to punish you. It's that I want you to win as well. I know you can.'

Natalie wasn't so sure, especially when Simon removed the brush and used his tongue instead. She felt his hot breath through the silk and her clitoris swelled with delight, throbbing relentlessly as her pleasure threatened to peak. Very gently he grazed the tip of it through the silk with his teeth and her hips jerked. 'Not yet!' he urged her.

By now Sajel was screaming aloud, crying out, not only with delight but also with terror because she was so close to coming. Her cries only heightened Natalie's excitement, and when she felt the Indian girl's body heaving desperately on the bed the first tingles of her own orgasm began to spread upwards through her body. 'I'm going to come,' she wailed. But as she spoke Sajel gave a cry of despair and then her body shook so violently that Natalie knew it was all over – and that she was the winner.

'Well done!' cried Simon. 'You can open your eyes now.' Natalie did, looking up at him as, clearly frantic with need himself, he roughly pushed the silk to one side and then plunged into her. At the same time he slid a hand beneath her and inserted a finger into her rectum.

Across the room she could hear the sound of latex against flesh and guessed that Sajel was being punished for losing. But by the sound of Sajel's cries the punishment was giving her even more pleasure. However, she knew that nothing could compare with the pleasure that Simon was giving her. For the first time ever, as he drove in and out of her and she felt herself spiralling into yet another dizzying climax, she believed that he was truly hers and that she was special to him.

After a few minutes Simon came too, and his cry of triumph sounded almost primitive. It was as though he was celebrating the fact that she was his, and that together they'd won.

For a few minutes there was silence in the room. 'I think we could do with another drink,' suggested Anil eventually. 'What about it, girls?'

Sajel looked as though she was going to protest, but then she and Natalie glanced at each other and smiled. There was no need for them to try and prove anything. It was possible that the men didn't understand it, but they both knew the truth. They held the balance of power because the men were enslaved by their obedience to them.

Once in the kitchen the two girls, both still naked except for the belts and silk scarves, fetched glasses and wine. 'How did your time away together go?' Natalie asked Sajel.

Sajel gave a secretive smile. 'It was wonderful, out of this world.'

'So you're going to give marriage a try?'

'I don't think either of us could ever be happy with anyone else. It's all thanks to The Haven, of course. How about you?'

Natalie told her briefly what had happened since they'd last met and how Simon was now working for her on the magazine. 'Isn't that a bit tricky?' asked Sajel.

'It's early days yet so I can't be sure. I think it's difficult for Simon when we're at work, but it's perfect for me all the time.'

'Well, that's the way it ought to be.'

'Yes. But we must never let them know what's happened as a result of our visit to The Haven, must we?' said Natalie.

'What do you mean?'

'Why, the fact that thanks to them we really have got it made. I'm happy at work, and I'm ecstatically happy here at home. I don't have any problem subjugating myself to Simon in order to get such incredible pleasure, and I haven't had to sacrifice anything. There's only one thing that I regret.'

'What's that?'

'That I can't share the secret of having it all with my

readership!' laughed Natalie. 'Come on, we'd better get the drinks back to the men. With any luck they won't have finished with us yet.'

Back in the bedroom the two men were talking earnestly together, and neither of them smiled when the girls walked into the room. Immediately Natalie felt the familiar, dark excitement stir within her once more. 'Why are you looking at us like that?'

'Because we now have another competition for you,' explained Anil.

'I don't think I can climax again yet,' lied Natalie.

'That's not for you to decide,' said Simon. Natalie averted her gaze so that he couldn't see the triumph in her eyes.

Clearly it was going to be as she and Sajel had hoped, and the night still held many more pleasures for them. Silently she thanked Jan for letting her know about The Haven and then, with her head bowed, she walked docilely towards Simon. She knew that he was watching her approvingly and she was trembling a little because she had no idea of what lay ahead.

However, what she *did* know was that at last she was completely satisfied with her life – and she was going to make sure that she kept Simon satisfied too. If she did then he probably wouldn't even need to continue working at The Haven because the pair of them, together with Anil and Sajel, could start their own group sessions. As the circle widened, their life would become so exciting that there wouldn't be time for The Haven in either of their lives again.

As Simon pulled Natalie's hands behind her back and fastened them with a pair of handcuffs, her breasts began to ache deliciously. And when his hands cupped their round fullness she knew that she really could – and, now, really did – have it all.